Strains

of

Music

Roberta Simpson Brown
&
Fatima S. Atchley

PublishAmerica
Baltimore

First printing

ISBN: 1-4137-4418-4
PUBLISHED BY PUBLISHAMERICA, LLLP
www.publishamerica.com
Baltimore

Printed in the United States of America

This book is dedicated to

Lonnie E. Brown
(musician extraordinaire)

and to the memory of

Ervin S. Atchley and Fran Palmer,

*all beloved family who brought
beauty, love, and harmony to our lives.*

We would like to thank the following for all their help and encouragement:

Heather Dotson, dear friend and computer whiz, who helped sort out and correct all the computer mistakes without laughing too much. We couldn't have done this without you!

Jane Jones, Marie Stewart, Alma Hood, and Wanda Waters, dear friends and caregivers who helped Fatima through the hardest part of her life after her stroke. Our family can never thank you enough for your devotion and dedication.

All friends and family members (especially Scott, Susan, Shawn, and Steven) who have said through the years, "Nana and Aunt Roberta, tell us a story!"

Chapter One

Nighttime didn't usually frighten Miss Fetney Lou. She liked to listen to the river sounds as she drifted off to sleep, but tonight it was the absence of these sounds that had awakened her. Tonight, she trembled. She recognized the stillness as a sign of danger.

She strained to hear anything that might reassure her that this was a normal night, but nothing came to her ears. Something was out there, though. For now it was only a feeling, but her senses never failed her in these things. She did not know what form evil would take this time, but eventually it would materialize.

"Why is it coming to Cajun Corners now?" she whispered, but, deep down, she already knew the answer.

Fetney Lou tossed and turned and waited for night to pass. She pulled the faded top quilt up as far as she could without affecting her breathing. She had done that as a child when she wanted to keep the creepie crawlies away.

She thought of lighting the lamp, but she was afraid that Oscoe might see it and think she was ill. She didn't want him coming over in the middle of the night to check on her. Not on this night anyway.

About two o'clock, she dozed. Her dreams were filled with

ghostly figures that flitted from tree to tree between her house and Silver Mist Plantation. They floated back toward her, and her own cries woke her. She lay waiting for morning, but it took its own good time coming.

The old woman was up at first light and saw the heron feeding in the swamp. She felt a strong kinship to the snowy bird. She, too, depended on the swamp to sustain her. Its sustenance had never been more important to her than on this day. The noises of the swamp had come to life and, in turn, revived her from the paralysis of fear that she had experienced from midnight on. She had almost forgotten what fear was like until last night.

The dream had haunted her through the waking hours until daybreak. She stood now, looking from her cabin to Silver Mist and watching for some sign that would give the dream meaning.

As Fetney Lou watched, she saw a figure emerge in the early morning mist among cypress trees and ancient stumps. At first, she thought she was dreaming again, but that wasn't true. This was no ghost or swamp creature. This figure was real. Fetney Lou moved closer, her steps silent and quick. She peered from behind the trees and saw that the low-water reflections showed a face framed by gold, shimmering in the water. Fetney Lou's heart jumped at the sight before her.

"She's come back," the old woman muttered. "Now that she's here, all the evil that's been festering will come to a head."

Fetney Lou remained camouflaged in the shadows and reflections of the black willows and wild flowers, wrapped in wisps of fog that still lingered in places near the water where the sun had not yet penetrated. She continued to watch as the golden lady stopped and stood at the point where Silver Mist Plantation joined the bayou, and looked at the long-dead giant cypress tree. Fetney Lou saw her move slightly to one side to get a better view of the opening in the great, hollow trunk.

Disturbed by the movement, the heron stopped its feeding and took flight. The golden lady, seeing it for the first time, reached out her hands as if to stop it. It was gone in a flash, soaring on the wind beyond her reach. She dropped her hands and stared sadly at the empty, hollow tree.

"Oh, Sheila," sighed Fetney Lou in a soft whisper. "You always did reach for the impossible."

The golden lady made no move to go, and Fetney Lou did not move either. Not even the keenest eye would be able to spot her. Fetney Lou shifted her gaze from the lady to the houseboat where Oscoe lived.

There was no sign of him, but that didn't mean he wasn't there. Fetney Lou knew him well, and had been able to track him in her mind for years. She knew he was up, and he would know this intruder had come.

A part of Fetney Lou longed to call out to Sheila, but she knew she could never do that. Shelia had made her choice, and Fetney Lou had not been part of it. She had always felt Sheila would come back someday, but she didn't know why she had left her world of glitter right now.

Fetney Lou gazed at the high spring water covering the twisted, dead stumps. She had always thought they had a quiet beauty all their own.

"Like your face, Sheila," she thought out loud, looking at the golden lady who was still in the same place. "You are beautiful on the surface, but you are twisted underneath just like these old, dead stumps. Your roots are here. You are part of all of this no matter how hard you try to cover it up."

Fetney Lou's thoughts were interrupted by the cry of a bird. She looked up, but the sky was empty. Only the sun's rays filtered down through the trees, turning the scene into a forest cathedral.

Fetney Lou looked back at her golden lady, but she had bowed her head and stood sobbing. Fetney Lou watched as she turned and ran toward Silver Mist. She watched until the figure was almost lost among the trees.

"Run," said Fetney Lou aloud, as if the retreating figure could hear her. "Run from the dead and the hand of God to a life more hollow than this old tree!"

She didn't watch Sheila completely out of sight. She had heard that was bad luck, and she wanted no more of that for either of them. She turned away and headed toward her own cabin.

As she moved along, the bird's cry came again. For an instant in their opposite headings, both the old woman and the young one hesitated long enough to look up. Backs turned toward each other, they watched as the white heron circled overhead. The bird flew out of sight, and the two women continued back to their own private worlds.

The strains of a melody drifted to Fetney Lou through the clear morning air. Sheila was singing a song Fetney Lou had never heard before, but she could only hear part of the words:

My mother was a snowy heron,
And like her, I will soar on the wind!

"Foolish girl!" muttered Fetney Lou.

The space between them widened and the separation continued, at least for a little while.

Observing unseen through the trees from his houseboat, Oscoe saw the whole thing. He shook his head and poured himself a cup of strong coffee to brace himself for the bad things yet to come.

Chapter Two

Kana's hands shook as she held the letter from her cousin Doug and his wife Nicole at Silver Mist. She knew that something unusual had happened to cause them to write. They always called instead of writing. She had ripped open the envelope as soon as she saw it and scanned the single page. Then she read it a second time slowly, making sure she didn't miss a word. She found the contents hard to believe. They had written because she had not responded to their call. She had no idea what they were talking about. She had not received a call or a message. That was strange. They said they had talked to Sheila about a week ago and asked her to give Kana the message. How could Sheila not tell her something so important? Could she have forgotten, or did she just not want her to know?

Kana had been too angry to look at the mail last night. It usually consisted of letters to Sheila from her fans. Sheila's secretary handled all the fan mail, but Sheila had asked Kana to do a daily screening process in case mail came from a relative or friend the secretary didn't recognize. Sheila wanted to see these personally. Last night Kana was so angry with Sheila, she had dumped the whole stack of mail without sorting it. She had faced the morning determined to sort out a lot of things. She'd decided to start with the mail. Her letter had been at the bottom of the stack.

After the second reading, Kana folded the letter and slipped it back into the envelope with the Cajun Corners postmark. Then she zipped it in her purse so she'd be sure to have it with her when she confronted Sheila later.

She reached for the phone to call Doug and Nicole at Silver Mist, but a glance at the clock told her it was too early. They would probably not be up for another hour. If they'd had a hard night with Great Pa, they'd need their sleep.

Four years ago, Doug and Nicole had moved into Silver Mist to take care of Great Pa Ulysses after his stroke. It was a mutual need fulfilled. Great Pa needed care, and Doug and Nicole had needed a place to start over after their only son had died in a fire that destroyed their home. Doug would inherit half of the estate anyway after Great Pa died.

It had been a long four years for everybody. In all that time, Great Pa had not spoken one word. Kana visited as often as she could, but traveling on the road with Sheila made it difficult. Doug and Nicole called with reports on Great Pa's condition so Kana would not have to wait for letters to catch up. Kana had been grateful to hear so often. She had been as close to Great Pa as she had been to her father. She had waited four long years to hear from Great Pa what had happened the day her father died, and she had about given up. Now the letter had come from Doug and Nicole, saying that Great Pa had been able to speak a few words and he was asking for Kana. Sheila had known this for over a week and hadn't told her. Kana couldn't understand why. Sheila knew how important it was to her. Kana felt almost as betrayed by this as she had by what happened last night. She felt the tears sting her eyes, but she blinked them back. She could not allow herself to cry. She had to depend on herself now. She didn't know anyone else to trust.

It hadn't always been this way. Kana remembered the days when she had lived at Silver Mist with her father and Great Pa. Sheila had been on the road then, too, but Kana had been busy with her father and didn't miss her that much. It had been exciting to hear about the places she had been when she did come home. Sheila always brought some small souvenir for Kana from each place. Sometimes she would sing to Kana. There was one tune she hummed over and over, but she never finished the words. Kana loved it and always asked to hear it before she went to sleep. She'd be asleep by the time Sheila sang the only two lines she'd written:

My mother was a snowy heron,
And like her, I will soar on the wind!

Kana would feel Sheila's lips brush her cheek even in sleep. She didn't know what Sheila's song meant, but she would dream of two snowy herons flying through a bright blue sky. When she'd wake in the morning, Sheila would be gone again. Kana would look at her souvenirs and wonder where her mother had gone this time. She'd hear the lines of the song in her head and try to figure out who Sheila's mother really was. Then there would be a knock on the door and her father or Great Pa would come in with a plan to fill the day.

It had been a long time since Kana had felt that loved. If the family felt the strain of Sheila's career in music, nobody ever mentioned it. Looking back, Kana was sure it had been hard on her father and Great Pa to be left with a child, but singing was what Sheila was born to do.

Then it all changed as suddenly and unexpectedly as the wind changes in the spring. There was no forecast to warn

Kana or to help her prepare for what was to come.

Everything seemed the same as always when Kana woke up that day. She had found her father's note on the table, telling her that he had gone into the swamp and would see her that afternoon. Great Pa was nowhere around, so Kana figured he must have gone with her father. She didn't learn until later that he had followed her father alone.

Kana made her own breakfast that morning. She toasted bread in the oven and fried two eggs. After she ate, she went up to her room to dress. She had just come back down to the kitchen to do the dishes when she heard voices outside. She looked out the window and saw the sheriff's car and a neighbor's truck in the driveway. They were lifting someone out of the truck and coming toward the house. Lord! Someone had been hurt! She dashed to the door and opened it. She looked down as the men walked by. It was Great Pa, pale and still.

"What happened?" cried Kana. "What's wrong with him? Somebody get my father!"

"Take him up to his room," the sheriff told the men. "It's the first room on the right, if I remember."

He looked at Kana. She nodded to confirm.

The men carried Great Pa up the stairs. Kana started to follow, but the sheriff's hand on her arm stopped her.

"Sit down, Kana," he said firmly.

Kana sat as ordered. Fear washed over her. She tried to will the sheriff not to speak, but she couldn't stop his words.

"I hate to tell you such bad news, Kana," he said. "Your father is dead. Your grandfather must have found him by that old hollow cypress in the swamp. The shock must have made him have a stroke. I've sent one of my men for the doctor."

"Oh, no!" sobbed Kana. "What happened to my father? He can't be dead! I want to see him!"

"Not now, child," said the sheriff. "Oscoe found both of them and came for me. We took your father to town and brought your grandfather home. He may be able to tell us what really happened. But until he can speak, we just don't know."

The sheriff's attention was drawn to the arrival of the doctor. As he went to let him in, Kana ran upstairs to her room and flung herself across the bed. This couldn't be happening! It had to be a terrible nightmare. Surely she would wake up and find things as they had been. But that had not been what happened at all.

Later, Kana remembered the doctor's voice outside Great Pa's room. After a while, he had come to her room. She was still crying, so he gave her something to make her sleep.

"What happened to my father?" Kana asked him.

"He was shot," the doctor answered.

"Shot?" she repeated. "Who would shoot my father? Everybody liked him! He never hurt anyone!"

The doctor repeated what the sheriff had already told her.

"Until your grandfather regains his speech, we just don't know. There were other tracks by the old tree, but we have no witnesses except your grandfather. Right now, he can't speak to tell us anything. I promise, I will let you know if we learn more. Now I want you to sleep."

Kana had drifted into a deep sleep then. When she woke, Sheila was sitting by her bed, and the morning sun was streaming through the window on Sheila's golden hair.

"We'll get though this somehow, Baby," she said.

Kana lived through the funeral in a daze. Her father

couldn't be gone! Surely she would go back home and hear him laughing like he always did at Silver Mist. Even when she touched his face and felt the coldness, she couldn't believe that wax-like face was really his.

Going back to Silver Mist had finally made Kana accept the reality of what had happened. The emptiness clung to her like a shroud she couldn't shake off. Questions crowded into her mind. Who had done this and why? How could she take care of Great Pa? She wasn't sure she could take care of herself! Her lifeline had been these two men.

She cried herself to sleep that night still wondering.

For the second time in two days, she woke to find Sheila sitting beside her bed.

Kana could see that she had been crying. For the first time since the funeral, Kana realized that Sheila was hurting, too.

When Sheila realized Kana was awake, she took her hand and smiled.

"I am taking you with me, Kana," she said. "I want you to pack as soon as you feel up to it. We'll leave tomorrow as soon as Doug and Nicole get here to take care of Great Pa."

The idea of leaving Silver Mist took Kana by surprise. Never in her wildest dreams did she think Sheila would take charge and take her away. Even though it would be good to get away from the memories of the last few days, it would be very hard to leave Great Pa. She had given him that name when she had learned to talk, because she thought he was the greatest grandfather in the world. He had always lived up to his title.

He had never let her down. He had made up for her not knowing her other grandfather.

She wondered if she should defy her mother and insist on staying at Silver Mist.

It was Doug and Nicole who convinced her that she should go. They promised to take good care of him, and Kana knew they would. Besides, she could visit often. During the past four years, she had gone whenever she could, even though great Pa never seemed to know she was there.

But now had come the stunning news that he could speak and was asking for her. Anger surged through her when she thought about Sheila knowing and not telling her! She wasn't going to get away with it! She was going to call Doug and Nicole and tell them she was leaving for Silver Mist right away.

"Hold on, Great Pa," she whispered aloud. "You've got to tell me what happened to you and Father! Don't die until I get there!"

She dialed with an urgency she couldn't explain. Maybe she was already too late!

Chapter Three

"You know, don't you?" asked Fetney Lou, as she handed a cup of strong black coffee to Oscoe. Her words were more of a statement than a question.

"Yes," he answered, nodding. "I saw her."

"We have no more time to waste," said Fetney Lou.

"No, I guess not," he agreed. "No more time. I kept hoping Kana's Great Pa Ulysses would come 'round enough to tell us what he saw that day. That may never happen though, and it's too dangerous to wait now that she's back. We will just have to act on what we believe to be true. It'll be hard on you, though, Fetney."

"It's always been hard on me," Fetney Lou answered, "but I'll survive. I always have."

She is a survivor, all right, Oscoe thought. *Not everyone is that strong, however.*

"What about Sheila?" he asked.

"She's brought it on herself," Fetney Lou replied. "She could stop all of this if she weren't so selfish. She never thought of the strains she put on others with her career! She never did care about anything but that infernal music. We can't stand by and watch Kana and Ulysses be destroyed."

"What do you want me to do?" Oscoe asked her. There

was no hesitation in his voice. He'd do whatever she asked of him, and he knew that she knew that.

Fetney Lou looked into his eyes, and each saw in the other a spark of the long abandoned love they had shared when they were young.

"What do you think is best?" she asked him.

"Bayou magic, maybe," he replied, shrugging. "Or maybe we should tell Joe Tarwater what we know and let him handle it. It's serious business we are mixing in, Fetney Lou."

"The outside world is too slow," she argued. "We have waited for four years, and we are still waiting. Nothing has been done by Joe Tarwater or the sheriff. Now we must look to ourselves and our own kind."

"Joe Tarwater is our own kind," Oscoe reminded her. "He's lived next to Silver Mist all of his life."

"But he works for the government now," said Fetney Lou. "He does things their way. We can't depend on him for this."

"I suppose you're right," Oscoe conceded. "We'll go ahead and do it your way."

"Good!" said Fetney Lou. "Then it's settled. Let's get started right now."

The old woman moved to the stove where she kept a pot of water boiling. From a wide wooden shelf beside the stove, she took down jars of herbs and the mandrake root she had gathered and stored. One by one, she dropped them into the boiling water and stirred them all together.

Oscoe knew the ritual well, but he watched her every move nevertheless. After all these years, she was still the most beautiful woman he ever saw, even though her hair was as white as the snowy heron she loved to watch.

"It's ready," she announced. "Help me with the rest,"

Oscoe took a match and a black candle from the metal box on the table. He struck the match and touched it to the wick. It caught and the flame flickered, casting menacing shadows around the room.

Fetney Lou reached again to the wide shelf and took down two dolls. *Kana and Great Pa!* She placed them beside the candle and sprinkled them with the bubbling mixture from the pot. Then she placed flowers beside them. *To frighten Kana away!*

Oscoe dropped two bubbles on the flame. The flame turned blue and almost died, but at the last second it caught and burned higher than before.

Fetney Lou and Oscoe joined hands and knelt before the candle. Together they began to chant their ancient prayers.

Deep in the swamp, the stillness was broken by the frightened cry of a snowy heron.

Chapter Four

Nicole answered Kana's call on the second ring.

"I'm sorry to call so early," Kana apologized, "but I just got your letter. How is Great Pa, Nicole?"

"He's very weak," Nicole replied, her voice edgy. "I don't know how much longer he can hold on."

"Nicole, I swear I didn't know until this morning," said Kana. "Sheila never gave me your message. You know I would have come if I had known Great Pa was asking for me!"

Kana heard Nicole gasp in surprise, but she recovered quickly. Her voice had lost its edge when she spoke again.

"Well, that explains it," she said. "I guess Sheila forgot, or maybe told someone else to give you the message."

"Maybe," said Kana. Kana didn't really think so, but there was no need to get Nicole in the middle of this. This was between Kana and Sheila.

"Can you come right away?" asked Nicole.

"I'm leaving this morning," said Kana. "Please tell Great Pa I'm coming."

"Great!" exclaimed Nicole. "We'll be expecting you. I'll tell Great Pa to hold on!"

Kana packed quickly. Most of her things stayed in

suitcases anyway since she had started traveling with Sheila. As she collected her watch and ring from the dresser, she noticed the tape she'd taken from Nat's office yesterday. She had forgotten all about it in the chaos of last night.

She picked it up and looked at the handwritten label. She still couldn't believe that Joe Tarwater would make a tape. In all the years she had lived next door to him at Silver Mist, he had never given her a hint that he was interested in a career in music. Yet when she had come back from lunch yesterday, there was Joe Tarwater right here in Nashville with Sheila's agent, Nat! She had only heard a snatch of the tape before Nat turned it off, but it had haunted her for the rest of the day. For some reason, it stirred memories of long ago at Silver Mist.

Joe had seemed surprised to see her when she walked into Nat's office. Maybe he was a little embarrassed that she might think he was using his acquaintance with Sheila to get into the music business like so many hopeful songwriters in Nashville did. Not that she would blame him. She had learned that you almost had to know somebody on the inside just to get your foot in the door. It was just that asking for help was out of character for the Joe Tarwater she knew.

She was glad she hadn't missed seeing him. She would have if she hadn't cut her lunch hour short to catch up on some work.

"Why didn't you let us know you were coming to town?" she asked him. "I could have shown you Nashville!"

"I'm only going to be here overnight. I'm on business for my regular job, but I thought I'd let Nat hear this tape on my lunch break," he explained.

It was the first time Kana had ever heard him talk so fast. He was uncomfortable, but Kana had no idea why he should be.

While they were talking, Nat removed the tape from the player and reached to put it in his desk drawer.

Kana made a quick decision. "Give it to me," she said, taking the tape before Nat could stop her. "I'll cut through the red tape and see that Sheila hears it."

"No need for that," Joe Tarwater protested.

Kana smiled. "I'd like to hear it myself."

Joe and Nat exchanged uneasy glances. Joe stood up and moved toward Kana. He reached out, attempting to reclaim the tape from Kana's hands. His fingers touched hers and Kana tingled at the unexpected pleasure she felt. Joe felt it, too. She saw it reflected in his eyes. She held tight to the tape until he let go. She didn't understand his reluctance to let her hear the tape, but it made her want to more than ever.

"Well!" he said. "I give up. My little tomboy friend still gets her way, even if she has grown up!"

He said goodbye to her and Nat, and left. Kana left, too, before Nat could do anything about taking back the tape. She had wanted time this morning to sit quietly alone and listen to it, and to try to figure out why a simple touch by somebody she'd always thought of as a friend could arouse such excitement in her! After all, she was still engaged to Jim Granger, even though after last night, that might not last long!

If her encounter with Joe had happened this morning instead of yesterday, she would have thought her reaction was in response to her anger toward Jim and Sheila.

But it had happened before she knew about them. She had responded to Joe because his touch had sent electrical shocks through her entire body. She had never felt anything like it. It was both the happiest and the most frightening moment of her life! Just thinking about it now, standing there holding the tape, brought back the powerful mixed feelings again.

She knew she'd have to calm down before she left for Silver Mist. She must clear her head to focus on driving. A cup of coffee would help. She could make a pot in the kitchen and listen to Joe's tape down there on one of the many tape players Sheila had installed all over the house.

As Kana reached the bottom of the stairs, she was surprised to see Sheila's tour bus parked in the driveway. As she crossed the large dining room between the hall and the kitchen, she smelled coffee already brewing. She moved closer. She could hear hushed voices, but she could not understand what they were saying. She pushed the door open, curious to see who was there. She was surprised. All of last night's anger came rushing back.

Charlie, Sheila's bus driver, and Jim Granger, her fiancée and Sheila's manager, were sitting at the table, half-asleep in spite of the steaming cups of coffee in front of them. Both became alert at the sight of Kana coming through the door. Neither spoke at first. Kana was speechless, too.

Thoughts were churning in Kana's head. *Sheila's bus! Sheila's driver! Sheila's house! Sheila's career! Sheila's manager! Sheila's everything! Jim Granger was mine! Why did she have to take him, too? Sheila's always got everything she wanted.* She choked back sobs. It just wasn't fair!

Kana realized she was still feeling the hurt and betrayal of last night. She had thought Jim was someone she had won on her own, but all Sheila had to do was snap her fingers and he went running to her. Kana wanted to run now and never see him again, but it was too late.

Jim stood up and pulled out a chair beside him at the table.

He motioned for her to join him.

"Come sit here, Kana," he said. "I know you're upset, but I want to explain about last night."

"What are you doing here?" she blurted.

Charlie was the one to answer.

"It wasn't my idea," he said. "Golden Girl wants us in Vegas! If you two will excuse me, I'll go get the bus ready to roll."

Kana wanted to stop Charlie, but he hurried from the room. She didn't want to be alone with Jim. She just wanted to get away and get to Great Pa, but she might as well get this over with now before she left. Then she could put it all behind her.

She held Joe's tape tightly as she crossed toward Jim. Her heart was beating so fast, she couldn't concentrate on what she wanted to say. Her mind was full of images of Silver Mist, Great Pa, and Joe Tarwater!

Chapter Five

Sheila stumbled through the trees that bordered Silver Mist, her breath coming in short gasps. She was visibly shaken by her visit to the old tree. The bayou breeze had rearranged her golden hair and left it hanging loose and out of place. Her head felt light, but her legs were heavy and jerked out of control.

She came to an old stump by the water and sat down on it to catch her breath. She dipped her hand in the water and splashed the cooling liquid on her face. She patted her cheeks and felt the soothing drops soak in. She repeated the process. Her head was clear now and her legs were beginning to feel normal again. She felt refreshed, but she made no move to go. She had never believed in the mumbo jumbo of Fetney Lou's magic, but she couldn't shake this sudden, deep sense of foreboding.

It was probably because she had gone to the old tree. From the moment she saw it, she knew it had been a mistake to come. All the pain came flooding back. She should have listened to Nat and Jim and done exactly what they told her to do.

"See how much the old man knows," Jim told her, "and find out if he's talked to anyone."

"And bring all the tapes and notebooks," Nat added. "I don't think you should leave them at Silver Mist anymore."

It would have been easier if she had followed their advice and then boarded her private jet to Vegas, but she couldn't bring herself to do it. Instead, she had gone to the old tree in the swamp to see it once more. She had to see where William Banet had died.

Sheila had truly loved William. Kana didn't believe that now, but William had known it. He had loved her, too, enough even to let her go fulfill her dream. And she had always come back to him when she could.

Letting her go freely was something her mother had never been able to do. She wanted to keep her tucked safely in a nest, protected from the world her father had come from and returned to. She had held Sheila back as long as she could, seeing traits of her father in her. Then Sheila had married William and had Kana, but it wasn't enough to hold her. Sheila had gone off to Nashville and become a star. Even though she had her husband's full support, her mother never forgave her for leaving.

It wasn't as if she never came back to see them! She did! And she knew it was better that way. She would have grown bitter if she had been forbidden to pursue her music. This way, when she was home between shows, she was happy to be with the family. She made the most of her time with them because she knew she did not have to stay forever. She was not trapped. She had her music to fill the rest of her time. It was the best of both worlds. At least, it had been until William had been killed four years ago. He had taken such good care of Kana. She had never shown any signs of her mother's wanderlust. She had been content to live at Silver Mist with William and Great Pa until William's death. If only things could have gone on as they were before that tragic day!

William had made everything good!

Sheila's mind drifted back twenty years to the first time she had met William Banet. It was a warm day with a hint of rain in the air. Sheila had slipped from the house with her guitar and walked barefoot to the cypress tree in the swamp. She loved it here!

This was her favorite place to go when she didn't want her mother to find her and give her chores to do. She wanted to sing!

And sing she did! She sang every song she had heard on the radio from the Grand Ole Opry! When she finished, someone had spoken from among the trees.

"I think the birds are jealous!" he'd said. "If they're not, they should be!"

Sheila had turned and seen William for the first time as he stepped from the shadows. Her heart had jumped a little as he approached her.

"My name is William Banet," he said. "My father, Ulysses Banet, just bought Silver Mist. My mother is dead, and I have no other relatives except my cousin Doug and his family in New Orleans. Now, do you know enough about me to marry me and sing for me the rest of my life?"

Shelia had laughed. Then he had laughed. He sat beside her and they talked. Then Sheila sang again. It had been like a glorious dream until her mother's voice had cut through the swamp.

"Sheila!" she called. "It's time for dinner!"

"I've got to go," she said. He only nodded. She could feel his dark eyes watching as she left him by the cypress. She knew her life would never be the same.

She had run through the swamp with her guitar, her blood surging hot and cold.

She reached the porch just as the rain began. She lay her guitar safely inside the door, and then she stood in the rain with her face upturned until the drops cooled the flushed, burning skin, like the swamp water had done just now. She had been eighteen, the same age as Kana now. That seemed like a lifetime ago!

She wished she could go back, but she had problems in the present to deal with.

Kana had been so angry last night! Sheila was afraid she had lost her forever. She had known she would have to pay a price for the lies, but she never meant to hurt Kana.

First, she had told the world that Kana was her sister instead of her daughter. When William died, Kana had only been fourteen. She couldn't leave her at Silver Mist, and she couldn't give up her career to stay at the plantation. She hadn't had time to think about the consequences of taking her on the road. Nat had pointed out that she couldn't suddenly present a half-grown daughter to her fans when they had never even been told she was married. Her youthful image sold records. She had to maintain it, so she had lied. That wasn't the lie that Sheila worried about the most, though. That lie had hurt Kana, but she understood. The lie Jim Granger forced her to tell last night hurt deeply, and there was nothing Sheila could do about it right now. Someday she would be able to tell Kana the truth about Jim. For now, she would have to live with Kana's anger and resentment. Sheila worried about Kana's reaction. She was headstrong like her. She couldn't predict what Kana might do.

Sheila had been very relieved that things had worked out

so well on the road up until now. Kana had adjusted to the change and had helped out in every way at first. Only once had she wanted to go back to live at Silver Mist, but Sheila had persuaded her that she needed her in Nashville. Of course, she would want to go back now with Great Pa asking for her, and Sheila couldn't allow that. It was too dangerous, but she couldn't tell Kana why. Kana was eighteen now. She could do as she pleased.

Sheila tried to explain to Jim that she couldn't stop Kana if she decided to move back, but he hadn't accepted that.

"If you can't control her, I can," he warned Sheila.

Sheila hadn't foreseen what method he would use. She was furious when he asked Kana out on a date. He only laughed when she confronted him about his motive. She then tried to convince Kana that Jim was too old for her, but Kana accused her of being jealous. Defeated, Sheila had backed off.

At least, dating Jim had put a stop to any thoughts Kana might have had about moving back to Silver Mist. Jim's marriage proposal had cinched it. Sheila would have to find a way to stop the marriage when the time came, but, for now, this situation seemed to be the lesser of two evils. Somehow she would find a way to get Jim Granger out of their lives forever.

Sheila shook her head, clearing all thoughts out of her mind. She reached again for the cool water, but something at the surface caught her eye. An alligator! And another one beside it! She shuddered! Were they looking at her? Of course not! That was crazy!

The foreboding intensified! She saw nothing but blackness and the big, toothy grins of the alligators.

"Get a grip, woman!" she said aloud. "You've seen

alligators before."

The darkness disappeared, but the feeling of doom persisted. It was closing in on her. She had to get away! She jumped up and ran for her life toward safer ground. Behind her, the alligators chomped on a different prey. Today Sheila had been lucky.

Chapter Six

Jim Granger poured steaming coffee into a cup and placed it in front of Kana. He was all charm as he smiled at her.

"Drink this," he said. "You'll feel better. Then we can talk."

"I don't want to talk," said Kana. "I just want to drink my coffee and listen to this tape."

Jim pulled the tape gently from her hand and placed it on the table. He knew Kana couldn't resist the coffee. He was right. She raised the steaming cup to her lips and sipped slowly. He waited until she had returned the cup to the table before he spoke.

"You can hear the tape later," he said. "I know last night was a bummer, but you owe it to me to let me explain."

Kana took another sip of coffee. She was beginning to feel calmer.

When Kana didn't speak, Jim went on.

"What happened last night was just a misunderstanding," he began. "The evening out with Sheila wasn't a real date. It was just publicity. I was only acting as her escort. I would have discussed it with you, but there wasn't time."

"I am not interested in anything you and Sheila do,"

Kana interrupted. "I have some thinking to do. I'm not sure how I feel about either one of you right now. I just want to hear Joe's tape and leave for Silver Mist."

Jim had thought that would probably be her plan. He had to delay her to be sure Sheila had time to get finished with all she had to do and get away from Silver Mist.

Jim was relieved that Kana had not yet heard the tape. He would have to think of some way to keep it now that he had gotten it away from her. He picked it up, pretending to be curious about the name on the label.

"Who is this Joe Tarwater?" he asked. He kept his voice casual and friendly. He had to play this carefully.

"A Cajun boy I grew up with," said Kana. "His family owned the plantation next to Silver Mist. We went fishing together sometimes, but he was older than I was . He had other interests. I never knew one of them was music until he brought this tape to Nat's office yesterday."

It didn't sound as if Kana had heard the conversation in the office between Nat and Joe Tarwater. That was one piece of luck in their favor.

"Didn't your friend let you know he was coming to town?" asked Jim.

"No," said Kana. "He wouldn't call me. I was only fourteen the last time he saw me. He still sees me that way. I guess he thought Sheila would be able to help him."

"Didn't you ever see him when you went back to visit at Silver Mist?" asked Jim.

"No," said Kana. "He went away to school before I left. Then he took some kind of job with the government. He came to Dad's funeral, but he's never been home when I was there after Dad's death. He was always a good friend."

"So you really don't know much about this guy now that

he's a man, do you?" asked Jim. "Maybe he's changed since you knew him."

"That's silly," said Kana. "Why are you asking me all these questions?"

"I'm not meaning to quiz you, Honey," Jim told her. "I just want to make sure this guy isn't trying to take advantage of you and Sheila."

"Joe would never do that!" Kana answered defensively.

"Once you're rich and famous, people come out of the woodwork trying to make a fast buck for themselves," said Jim.

"Joe was as sweet as ever yesterday," Kana answered.

She felt herself blushing, but Jim gave no indication that he noticed. Certainly, he did notice. He couldn't afford to have this Tarwater guy come in and spoil his set up. Of course, he had only made a play for Kana to keep her under his control, but he couldn't let her suspect that just yet.

"Look, Baby," he said, softening his voice, "I guess I'm a little jealous when some guy gets your attention. You know how much I care for you."

"You didn't seem to care much about me last night," Kana retorted.

Jim decided to let that remark pass and concentrate on exploring Kana's feelings for Joe Tarwater a little more.

"I truly don't want you to be hurt," he said smoothly. "You are very young and vulnerable right now. I'm trying to look out for you. I just want you to be careful. You are so beautiful! You'll meet all kinds of guys trying to take advantage of you."

"Are you trying to take advantage of me, Jim?" asked Kana.

"How can you say that?" he replied. "I love you! I've

asked you to marry me, Baby!"

"I'm not a baby," snapped Kana, "and Joe Tarwater is not trying to take advantage of me. I took the tape yesterday. He didn't ask me to. In fact, I got the feeling he didn't even want me to! He didn't know I would be at Nat's office when he brought the tape in. But let me tell you, Jim Granger, if he asks for my help in any way, he'll get it one hundred per cent!"

Kana slammed her coffee cup down on the table. Before Jim could reply to her outburst, Charlie walked back in.

"The bus is ready to roll, Jim," he said. "Are you coming?"

In one sweep, Jim slipped the tape into his coat pocket and moved around the table to Kana. He bent and kissed her cheek quickly and followed Charlie toward the door.

"You're right, Kana," he said over his shoulder. "I was wrong to say those things about your friend. I'll give this tape to Sheila myself as soon as we get to Vegas. If the guy has talent, we'll help him all we can."

"But–," said Kana, jumping up from her chair.

"Get some rest, sweetheart," Jim called to her. "I'll phone you from Vegas!"

"Wait!" shouted Kana. But the two men were already boarding the bus. Jim blew her a kiss from the window as the bus pulled out.

Kana sat back down and leaned her elbows on the table. Maybe she did need somebody to take care of her, but certainly not Jim Granger. He had been different this morning. She felt he was up to something, and she couldn't trust him. Why hadn't she seen how slick he was before? He had just walked out with a tape she had wanted very much to hear, and she couldn't shake the feeling that his reason for taking the tape wasn't to help Joe Tarwater! She stared at her empty cup, confused.

"What else don't I know?" she asked, but the empty cup had no answer.

Chapter Seven

Oscoe sat in his favorite chair and felt the gentle rocking of his houseboat on the water. From his small window, he could see the branches along the river bowing low in the wind. A storm was brewing, no doubt. Oscoe didn't mind. He liked a good storm.

He had left Fetney Lou's cabin after they had finished the ritual. He knew she'd want to be alone after that. He needed some time alone himself, even though being alone with his thoughts was sometimes painful in spite of all the years that were supposed to heal. No, time did not cure all.

He let his mind drift back, lulled by the soothing movement of the boat. It was hard to imagine any world other than the one he occupied now, but he remembered how the other world had intruded and destroyed his dreams. The outside world was ready to strike again. What would it destroy this time?

His dreams had once been centered on Fetney Lou. He could still picture her as a beautiful young woman and himself as a handsome young man. God, how they'd loved each other once!

He had come to the swamp to study it. He was going to write a book! He chuckled aloud as he remembered. He had bought a houseboat and anchored it on the river near Cajun Corners.

He had hurried to the swamp that first morning to sketch the snowy heron in the first light. He had made the last stroke when he felt someone watching him. He turned and saw Fetney Lou for the first time.

He smiled, and a faint smile crossed her lips in return. She kept her distance like the other wild creatures.

"Stay there," he said. "I want to sketch you."

She had stayed. He tried as hard as he could, using all his training and natural talent, but he could not make her as beautiful as she really was. Finally, he finished.

"Can I see?" she asked.

He held up the sketch and she came closer. A wider smile crossed her face this time.

"Am I really that pretty?" she asked.

"Prettier," he assured her. "Much, much prettier! I wasn't able to do you justice!"

"Momma says it's wrong for a person to think about their looks," she said.

"Then I'll think about them for you," he laughed.

That had been the beginning. He'd go into the swamp to observe the wildlife and sketch for his book. Fetney Lou would appear from nowhere it seemed and watch quietly until he finished. Then they would sit and talk.

"Papa drowned during a storm on the river," Fetney Lou revealed. "Momma got a settlement and we've lived off that. It's hard, though. When Momma's drinking, she doesn't buy much food."

Oscoe made up his mind to take Fetney Lou away from the swamp to a better life. They made such plans! They would get married and live in a real house. They would have children, and Oscoe would have the family he had missed in foster homes.

Maybe he had wanted it too much. Maybe that was why it was never meant to be.

He remembered the day it happened. He had just finished breakfast and was collecting his sketchbook and supplies when Fetney Lou had pounded on the door.

"Oscoe, come quick! It's Momma! She's bleeding!" she sobbed.

Oscoe had dropped everything and raced after her through the swamp. The cabin was neat except for the clutter of bottles around the woman's bed. Blood, the color of coffee grounds, had soaked the bedding.

"She's hemorrhaged from the stomach," he told Fetney Lou. "We'll have to get her to a doctor."

Oscoe carried her outside and put her in the boat. The river carried them to town.

Fetney Lou cried quietly. "It's all that drinking! I told her it would kill her!"

Oscoe remembered how the doctor had shook his head.

"I'll do what I can," he'd said, "but it doesn't look good. She'll have to stay in the hospital for a while."

"Go on home," Fetney Lou had told him. "I'll have to stay with her. She won't want to stay alone."

Reluctantly, he had gone. The swamp, though teeming with life, seemed empty without Fetney Lou. He hurried to finish his book. It took his mind off the terrible loneliness he felt. He made the trip in his small boat to the hospital to check on Fetney Lou and her mother, and to show Fetney Lou his completed manuscript. He should have noticed it then. There were signs of it coming. He saw the flushed cheeks and the loss of innocence in her eyes, but he thought the change in her was caused by the ordeal she was enduring. She was preoccupied when he explained that he would be going away for a few weeks to see publishers.

"Take all the time you need," she said. "That'll be fine."

He had gone, but in the end, it hadn't been fine at all. The publishing part was good. He had found a publisher who wanted the book! He called the hospital to tell Fetney Lou the good news, only to learn that her mother had hemorrhaged again and died. One of the doctors had taken Fetney Lou home.

Oscoe hurried back and went straight to Fetney Lou's cabin. The doctor was still with her. She was packing her clothes and the doctor was boarding up the cabin. Oscoe was amazed!

"What's going on?" asked Oscoe. "What are you doing?"

"I'm leaving," said Fetney Lou, without meeting his eyes.

"Why?" asked Oscoe, totally bewildered. "Where are you going? How will you live? I thought you loved this place. I thought you loved me!"

Fetney Lou stopped her packing and faced him. "I do love this place and you, but I am not going to die penniless like my mother." She stopped and looked at the man who was still boarding up her old home. She looked back at Oscoe and continued. "He can give me everything I've ever wanted. I never realized there was so much out there in the real world. And he loves me, Oscoe. If you love me as much as you say you do, you'll let me go! You'll want me to have a better life."

Oscoe was paralyzed with pain. Without a word, he turned and stumbled home.

He sat for hours, staring out across the swamp. She couldn't be going out of his life forever. He had to talk to her. Maybe he could convince her to stay. He hurried back to her cabin, but when he got there, it was deserted. She had already gone.

In the months that followed, Oscoe experienced hell, pure and simple. At first, there was disbelief.

"How could she do this to me?" he asked over and over to everything he saw.

Then he became angry! He thought of her in the stranger's arms, and he remembered all the times he had held her and wanted her, but made himself wait.

Then came acceptance, but the loss was almost unbearable. In the end, he knew he loved her and would always love her no matter what! He was better for having loved her. He would go on with his life.

His first book sold well, and his publisher asked for second one. Work was his salvation. He spent his waking hours sketching and writing.

One morning when he had gone out to sketch in the early light, he saw smoke rising from Fetney Lou's old cabin. He ran through the swamp and saw Fetney Lou with a stranger. This one was very small! It was a baby girl!

"Oscoe, this is my daughter, Sheila," she said.

"Is your husband with you?" asked Oscoe.

"I have no husband," she answered. "He was married. He never meant to marry me at all. I've been a fool."

"Marry me," Oscoe said quietly. "I'll take care of you and Sheila."

Fetney Lou's eyes filled with tears.

"I can't now," she said.

"Why not?" he asked. "I'm making lots of money from my book now. I can give you all the things you want."

"You deserve better than me," she said.

Oscoe sensed both her pride and her shame, and he knew

it would be useless to ask again. But if she had chosen to stay here, then so would he. At least he would be near her.

He had stayed like a sentinel, guarding her and the child. He had watched the years turn her hair the color of the snowy heron she loved to watch. He had been proud that he had been able to help her and Sheila through the years, but he was powerless to help now.

He watched the summer storm come and go. He prayed the coming trouble would come and go as fast.

Sheila's face showed no trace of tears by the time she reached Silver Mist. Nicole was sitting at the table drinking coffee when Sheila came in. Sheila poured herself a cup and joined Nicole at the table. Nicole's look was not a welcoming one. Sheila ignored it.

"Is Great Pa awake?" she asked Nicole.

"No, he's asleep," Nicole replied curtly. "Doug's with him now."

"I'll look in on him before I go," said Sheila.

"It's Kana he's asking for," Nicole told her. "Why didn't you give her our message?"

"I didn't want to get her hopes up until I checked on his condition myself," said Sheila. "She's been through a lot, and I don't want her upset."

"She'd be more upset if Great Pa died without telling her what she's been waiting to hear all these years," said Nicole.

"What do you think he'll say?" asked Sheila. "What could he possibly know about what happened?"

"You'd know more about that than I would," Nicole replied sharply. "If you had been home with your husband and child instead off somewhere with your music, maybe none of this would have happened."

"Ah!" Sheila shot back. "Spoken like the dutiful wife! I

know you don't approve of my lifestyle, but it's really none of your business!"

The two women glared at each other across the table. Nicole knew Sheila was right. It was none of her business. She rose, set her cup in the sink, and left the room.

Sheila smiled to herself. So what if Nicole disapproved of the way she lived? She wasn't about to let her interfere with what she had come here to do. She wasn't the one who was intruding. Silver Mist had been her home long before Nicole had moved in. She wondered if Nicole had gone straight up to complain to Doug. Maybe it would be best to go on up now and see the old man.

Sheila climbed the stairs and stopped outside Great Pa's door. It was partially open and she could see Great Pa on the bed. His breathing was even, but he was pale.

Doug looked up as she entered, but he made no move to leave.

"I'll sit with him a while," offered Sheila. "You can take a break or get some breakfast."

"Thanks, but I've had breakfast," Doug replied. His voice was somewhat cold, but Sheila pretended not to notice.

"Then you can stretch your legs. You must be tired," she said sweetly.

Doug remained by the old man's bed.

"I don't need to stretch my legs," he insisted.

"Then do it anyway!" snapped Sheila. Her sweetness was gone now. Her eyes glittered and her jaw was set with determination. "He's my father-in-law! I have a right to see him alone if I want to!"

Doug stubbornly held his ground.

"You don't have any more rights than anyone else in this house, Sheila!" he told her. "You may own most of Nashville, but you don't own Silver Mist! It belongs to Great Pa as long as he lives, and I intend to see that he stays alive a long time!"

"You surely don't think I've come to kill him, do you?" Sheila asked, her voice rising.

"Of course not!" said Doug, calming down. "I just don't like it when you try to keep Kana away from him."

"Doug, you know I've got to protect her," said Sheila. "She loves this place and Great Pa very much. The situation here could hurt her terribly."

"You can't keep her away from here forever," said Doug, "especially since he's asking for her."

As if on cue, the old man on the bed moaned and opened his eyes.

"Kana," he said, his words barely audible. "Mar–"
Doug and Sheila rushed to his side.

"What is it?" asked Sheila. "What is it you want to tell us?"

"Kana," he repeated, struggling with the words. "Mar–"
The effort was too much. He closed his eyes and slept again.

"You see!" hissed Sheila. "You know what he's trying to say, don't you? He'll try to tell Kana if she comes! We can't let her get mixed up in this, Doug! You've got to help me protect her! He might be able to make her understand what he is saying, and you know how she would react to that!"

"Maybe it would be better if he did," said Doug sadly. "Then maybe this could all be over."

"Don't be a fool," warned Sheila. "If she finds out what's going on at Silver Mist, it could ruin us all."

"Maybe," said Doug, "but –"

"Besides," Sheila cut in, "we don't know how much he knows. We don't know who the killer was, and if he tells

Kana, it could put her life in danger!"

The old man stirred at the sound of their voices, but he made no renewed effort to speak.

"I can't deny her a last chance to see her grandfather," said Doug. "So far, he's only said that one thing over and over. Kana would never be able to connect that with her father's death."

"You'd better make sure she doesn't!" said Sheila. "I'll hold you responsible for Kana's safety if she comes here."

Her emotions spent, Sheila left Doug with Great Pa and went directly to the room she had shared with William. The room was kept ready for her whenever she came home.

She took down the picture that covered the wall safe and opened the combination lock. She took one of William's notebooks and packed it at the bottom of her suitcase. She closed the safe and replaced the picture. The supply of notebooks was diminishing fast, but she didn't want to remove all of them at once. They were safer here for now. When the supply ran out, she would deal with it then. She grabbed her suitcase and headed for the airport. She should be able to slip into Vegas unnoticed. Nobody would suspect she had made a stop at Silver Mist.

Airborne, Sheila's private jet, The Snowy Heron, climbed above the clouds, banked, and headed on a straight and level flight to Las Vegas. Sheila unfastened her seat belt and took down her suitcase. She took out William's notebook and flipped through the pages. What would her fans do if they found out? Fame could be so fickle. She would die without it. She had to hold on for now. That meant she had to keep her secret.

Chapter Eight

Kana did not know that Sheila was in the skies over Cajun Corners. She had assumed that Sheila had flown directly to Las Vegas for her next show after their fight last night.

Kana was no longer angry this morning. She had been very immature last night, but she was seeing things differently now. Maybe one could grow up overnight! She recognized that the change in her had come about because of the feelings she had for Joe Tarwater that still lingered on after their chance meeting yesterday. That was the reason she saw Jim in a different way this morning. Maybe Sheila had just needed Jim to escort her to the awards last night after all. Kana was embarrassed when she thought about the jealous fit she threw when she saw them together at the party. Thank goodness, she had done it in private. She wondered now if she had really cared that much or if she was unconsciously looking for a reason to break up with Jim. She knew herself well enough to know that she sometimes got angry when she didn't know what else to do.

She glanced at the headline in the morning paper: "Superstar Sheila Banet Walks Away With Everything!" There was a picture of Sheila smiling up at Jim. The sight of that didn't hurt as much this morning as it had last night when Sheila had told her she couldn't go to the awards dinner. Kana didn't care about Sheila's awards or her image anymore. She just longed for a real family again.

Kana remembered how exciting it had been to think of Sheila traveling all over the country when she lived at Silver Mist with her father and Great Pa. She had roots!

The tragic death of her father had changed that without warning. She'd had no choice then about her life. Now she did. Now it was time to go back. She had never driven from Tennessee to Louisiana by herself before, but she knew she could do it now. She was eighteen now and all grown up. As she started to her room to get her things together for her trip, a little voice inside her head reminded her that growing up could be a very scary thing!

Chapter Nine

Joe Tarwater paced the floor of his hotel room in downtown Nashville. He'd been awake most of the night trying to decide what to do about the tape. He had never intended for Kana to hear the songs. He would never want to put her in danger, but it could happen if he didn't get the tape back. Of course, he had copies, but he wanted the one Kana had.

If she heard it, she might remember the music. He'd played it for Nat so he and Sheila would know that he was on to what was going on. He had deliberately waited until noon to go to Nat's office because he thought Kana would be out to lunch.

"Rats!" he said loudly, popping his fist in his hand. "Why did she have to come back early?"

Not that he hadn't been glad to see her! It was a jolt to see her so grown up. Four years had made a drastic change. She had been a cute tomboy, but now she was a beautiful young woman. He hadn't been able to get her out of his thoughts since their hands touched yesterday. He reached for the phone several times to call her, but each time he had talked himself out of it. He was too old for her. But then again, six years wasn't such a big difference now!

Joe hoped Kana hadn't had time to listen to the tape. Last night would have been hectic with the awards dinner and all. Maybe she had put it off until today. Everything would have been fine if his plan to be in and out of Nat's office during lunch had worked.

Nat would have listened to the tape and persuaded Sheila to go public and forget the blackmail. Then the trouble at Silver Mist could end without anyone getting hurt.

Right now, he would like to tell Kana that Jim Granger was a crook and a creep, and order her to pack her bags and come home with him to Cajun Corners. But, of course, he couldn't reveal such information now. He still had an assignment to complete. But a trip to Cajun Corners was another matter. He was going home and she would be going to Silver Mist to visit Great Pa. He decided to take a cold shower and then place a call to Kana.

Chapter Ten

Kana was glad Sheila was gone. She wasn't angry with her anymore, but she wasn't ready to face her either. She was proud that Sheila had won the awards last night, but she wasn't in the mood to tell her yet.

Kana knew how hard Sheila had worked to be a country music superstar. It hadn't been as easy as it looked. She had sung in clubs and played one-night stands and gigs in every little dive across the country. She had appeared at drive-ins, festivals, business openings, smoky bars, county fairs, and barn dances. She had refused to give up! Then she won a contest and a recording contract! William drove her to Nashville himself!

When she got her first big hit, most people thought it had just happened overnight!

How lucky she was, they said! But Kana knew that luck had not been the reason at all!

Sheila deserved to be recognized for her talent and the sacrifices she had made to get to the top in such a competitive business, especially with nobody on the inside pulling for her. Kana didn't want to take away from that, but she did wish to be recognized as her daughter.

Kana picked up the picture she always kept of Sheila and

placed it in her suitcase on top of her other things. This had been William's favorite picture of Sheila. She was smiling from a gold frame, her head tilted just right to catch the light on her golden blond hair that fell over her shoulders. The sequins glittered on the fancy blue western outfit. It made Kana feel homesick for her father and Great Pa and the life she had once had with them at Silver Mist.

Kana closed the suitcase and studied her own face in the mirror. She didn't have her mother's golden glitter, but the face reflected back to her was certainly nothing to be ashamed of. She had the dark good looks of her Cajun father. Maybe that was why he had always been so proud of her.

She had never felt that Sheila shared that pride. She always wanted Sheila to tell the world, "Hey! This little girl is mine!" But it never happened. Kana couldn't understand that. Other big female stars like Dottie and Tammy and Loretta even took their children on stage sometimes for the whole world to see. Kana didn't care about going on stage. She wanted people to know who she was! Sheila explained that it had to do with maintaining the image that would sell the most recordings. Fans thought she was young and single, so that's what she pretended to be. Kana didn't know about images and sales. She just knew she needed her mother to love her.

She wondered if this need had caused her to get involved with Jim Granger. Her relationship with him gave her a new identity. She had liked that at first. Last night was a real eye-opener, however. She tried to picture Jim in her future, but she couldn't! She realized that she couldn't even picture his face! *You couldn't be in love with somebody if you couldn't even remember what they looked like when they'd been gone such a short time, could you?*

Her thoughts were interrupted by the phone. She lifted the receiver and said hello.

She was afraid she'd hear Jim or Sheila on the line, but Joe Tarwater's good morning was like a caress. His voice excited her, and her hand on the receiver began to shake.

"Kana, I had an idea, "said Joe. "I wanted to see what you think about it."

When Kana hung up the phone a few minutes later, Jim Granger was the farthest thing from her mind!

Chapter Eleven

The Snowy Heron circled the Las Vegas airport in a holding pattern. Sheila didn't mind the delay this time. She needed more time to think about the material she was going to use in her next recording session. Right after Las Vegas, she would have to hurry back to the studio in Nashville.

It was important to get a new hit right away even after winning all the awards last night. Reporters would be asking about her next project. She couldn't tell them she had nothing in the works! Superstars didn't stay on top anymore by past glory and one-hit-wonders! They had to produce new and better material all the time.

She looked through William's notebook again. There was enough material there for two sessions, but she'd have to spread them out and make them last now that William was dead. Either that or take a chance on using her own songs. She didn't have enough confidence in her writing ability to do that just yet.

There was a time early in her career when she had honestly intended to tell the world that it was her husband and not she who wrote her hit songs. They seemed to flow so effortlessly from William, but he wanted no part of the spotlight. Nat was delighted with that. He encouraged

Sheila to stay with the single image, so it was difficult to change once the deceit was started. She convinced herself that it really didn't matter who got credit since it was all in the family anyway. William was happy to fill notebook after notebook with words and music. Sheila put them on tape so he could listen when she was gone. He had Kana and she had her career. They were both satisfied.

"I wasn't kidding," he'd laugh and say, "when I told you I wanted you to marry me and sing for me forever!"

But he had died! And things had changed so quickly!

Jim Granger had been the young attorney appointed by his firm to handle all of William's affairs. He'd only been with the firm a short time before William's death, and William had never had any reason to distrust him. Jim had found out about Sheila and Kana, and he discovered that William actually wrote the songs that Sheila took credit for. After William's death, Jim lost no time in approaching Sheila with the threat of exposure is she didn't go along with his plans.

Jim Granger's price for silence had been a high one, and, in the end, Sheila had paid it. It was the easiest thing to do. Jim was to become her business manager as a front for his illegal operations at Silver Mist. Even though Silver Mist belonged to Great Pa technically, it was still Kana's home. Great Pa would one day leave it to her and Doug, but he was much too ill to oversee what was going on there now. Doug would be powerless to do anything without hurting Kana and Great Pa. Jim threatened to make it look like the whole Banet family had been part of making Silver Mist a drug center. People would believe a lawyer. They would be willing to believe Sheila was into drugs because she was into music! And if they found out that William was the one who wrote her songs, that evidence of fraud would go to support his story. Sheila's fans would not be so loyal if her wholesome image was destroyed, and she would lose everything! She accepted his deal and vowed to find a way to expose him later.

Sheila never dreamed that things could get any worse. She had no way of knowing that Jim would pull Kana personally into his plans. She had tried to protect her. She had taken her away from Silver Mist as soon as Jim had started his operation there.

That had been a mistake, too. She had exposed her to Jim on the road and now they were engaged! She had to find a way out of this! She had to!

Lately, Sheila had begun to wonder if Jim Granger had had something to do with William's death. Maybe he tried to blackmail William in the short time he worked for him, and maybe William said no. He had certainly kept Kana away from Jim. They had never met until after William died. When Sheila agreed to make Jim her business manager, she had explained to Kana that she needed legal assistance to run her career now that William was gone. Nat was busy as her agent and didn't have the time nor the expertise to manage the financial side. Kana had accepted that.

It hadn't been so easy to convince Nat to go along, but he hadn't been able to think of a way out either. In the end, he went along against his better judgment.

Lately, Sheila had also begun to fear that Jim might have ideas of doing away with her and Kana. If he married Kana, he could get control of everything. He could arrange some kind of accident for Sheila and Kana and get all of their money.

Sheila had tried hard to keep Kana from finding out what was happening at Silver Mist. She knew her daughter well enough to know that she would go straight to the police. She would never stand for Silver Mist to be used like that, especially with Great Pa still there.

That was why she couldn't give Kana the message that Great Pa was asking for her. Kana would let nothing stop her from going to his side once she knew he was now able to speak even a few words. It was dangerous to go to Silver Mist now. It had been foolish of Nicole and Doug to call her.

It was dangerous, too, for Kana to remain engaged to Jim Granger. Sheila had hoped to find a way to convince Kana to break the engagement on her own. She had staged the scene last night to make Kana angry with both of them. Kana would probably hate her, but at least she would be free of that horrible man to some extent. She hoped that someday she would be able to explain her motives to Kana and that she would understand.

The pilot's voice announced over the speaker that The Snowy Heron had been cleared to land. The plane began its final descent. Sheila felt like she was descending into hell.

Chapter Twelve

Kana's heart was pounding as she hung up the phone. She danced joyfully around the room, hugging herself! She was going to Cajun Corners with Joe Tarwater! And it had been his idea! She couldn't believe her luck. Now she wouldn't have to drive alone, and she would have the whole day alone with Joe! Maybe she was excited about Joe after all these years because she was breaking up with Jim, but she didn't think so. This wasn't someone she had met on the rebound.

She and Joe had known each other all their lives. When she was six and he was twelve, he had sometimes taken her fishing. He'd been like a big brother, but he never treated her like a baby. At twelve, she had still been a tomboy when he finished school and went away. Two years later, he had come home for her father's funeral. She remembered that he had held her that day for the first time and let her cry, and he'd told her he was sorry.

"Somebody will pay for this, Kana," he had promised her. Then he had gone away again.

She hadn't thought about Joe in the days that followed. She lived in a world of hazy pain, even after Sheila took her on the road. She thought of the cruelty that had been inflicted on the two people she loved most. In a way, Great Pa had died as surely as her father. The stroke had left Great Pa's body like a coffin holding the stricken man. She wondered what it was like for Great Pa in his speechless, inactive world. *Could he hear, or was it a silent world, too?*

She looked around the room to see if she had packed everything she needed. She looked at her hand and slipped Jim's ring from her finger. She unzipped a small compartment in her purse and dropped the ring inside. She would give it back to Jim the next time she saw him. Even though she hadn't officially broken the engagement and returned the ring, it was over right now as far as she was concerned. She was free, and it felt absolutely wonderful! She felt good about making this decision on her own.

Jim was always making decisions for her. He decided where they would go, what she would wear, and what she should buy. He'd even taken Joe's tape to Sheila without letting her hear it!

When Joe called, he had asked her if she had heard the tape. She was sorry to have to tell him she hadn't. She thought he might be upset, but he wasn't. It was odd, but she thought he uttered a sigh of relief. He was probably embarrassed for her to know that he had come to Sheila for help.

Kana took one more look around the room. The clock reminded her that she needed to get dressed if she was going to be ready when Joe arrived. She looked carefully through her closet. She didn't want to look like a tomboy today. She selected a light green dress that had drawn compliments when she'd worn it before. She dressed quickly and gave herself a final inspection. She hoped Joe liked green. She felt like dancing around the room again, but the ringing of the phone stopped her. Maybe Joe was calling to tell her he was going to be late or that he had changed his mind about going. She hoped not! She snatched up the phone on the third ring!

"Hello!" she said breathlessly.

"Hello, Baby!" a familiar voice said.

Jim Granger's voice took her by surprise. She hadn't expected him to call her so soon.

"Oh," she said, the disappointment showing in her voice. "Hello, Jim."

"Is something wrong, Kana?" he asked smoothly. "You surely aren't still angry with me."

"No," said Kana, "I'm not angry anymore. I just wasn't expecting you to call right now."

"I just wanted to make sure you are okay. I'm sorry about leaving so abruptly," he said.

"It doesn't matter," Kana replied. "I think we said all we had to say, except one thing."

"What's that?" asked Jim.

"I might as well tell you now," said Kana, thinking it would be easier to say if she didn't have to tell him face to face. "I'm breaking our engagement. I'll return your ring as soon as I see you."

"Kana!" said Jim. "You can't mean that! You're just upset! I'll fly back as soon as I can and we'll talk all this out. Until then, I'm going to pretend the conversation never took place!"

Kana heard the phone click before she could say another word. Kana thought how typical that was of Jim. He would make a statement and just end a discussion. Whatever he had to say would make no difference this time. Her mind was made up.

The doorbell rang downstairs, and Kana's thoughts shifted to the trip ahead. She grabbed her bags and ran to the front hall where Joe Tarwater was waiting.

Chapter Thirteen

Joe carried Kana's bags and put them in the car. Then he opened the door and moved a stack of papers from the seat on the passenger's side.

"Sorry," he smiled. "I'm used to traveling alone. I use the car as an office most of the time. I can't let you sit on dirty papers and mess up that pretty green dress!"

Kana smiled back. His comment had made dressing up worth the effort. Maybe her tomboy look would be a thing of the past. Sitting beside Joe, driving down Music Row, Kana thought it might be a good time to approach him about the tape.

"I was planning to listen to your tape this morning," she began, "but Jim and Charlie were leaving for Vegas and Jim insisted on taking it to Sheila personally."

"I don't think you would have liked what you heard," Joe answered. Kana caught a hint of grimness in his voice.

"Maybe I can have a personal concert on the way," Kana suggested.

Joe pulled on to the interstate. Then he glanced at Kana and smiled.

"I'd much rather hear about you," he said. "We have a lot of catching up to do. Tell me what's been going on with you."

"I just broke my engagement to Jim Granger on the phone right after you called," said Kana, surprised at her need to start with that revelation.

"Good!" said Joe.

"Good?" repeated Kana, surprised.

"Yes, good!" Joe repeated. "Does it surprise you that I'd say that?"

"Frankly, yes! A little," said Kana. "Most people would say 'sorry'."

"I give honest answers, " said Joe, flashing a quick grin.

"Why did you say that? Do you know Jim?" she asked. "Don't you like him?"

"Doesn't matter," said Joe. "A pretty young girl like you shouldn't marry the first man who asks her."

Kana felt her cheeks burning. She hadn't blushed in a long time.

"What if no other man asks?" she teased.

"Don't worry," said Joe. "I'm sure one will."

They both laughed and drove on for a while in a comfortable silence.

Kana was happy to be on her way home. She wondered how Great Pa was doing right now.

"Did you see Great Pa before you came to Nashville?" she asked, breaking the silence.

"No, just Oscoe and Fetney Lou," he answered. "They told me your grandfather was able to say a few words."

"He's been asking for me, but Sheila didn't give me the message," Kana told him. "I wouldn't have known if Doug and Nicole hadn't sent me a letter. I'll never forgive Sheila if Great Pa dies without telling me what he wants me to know."

"Just one word of caution, Kana," Joe said seriously. "Don't expect too much."

"What do you mean?" asked Kana, feeling a little flurry of fear go up her spine.

"Just that things are sometimes not what we expect them to be," he said.

"I don't understand," said Kana.

"He may just ramble and make no sense. He may not have anything to tell you about your father, you know," Joe explained.

"Yes, I know," Kana admitted. "Then again, maybe he might!"

"Sometimes old people can take a turn for the worse fast," said Joe. "He might not be able to speak at all by the time we get there."

"I know that, too," said Kana, "but he's been saying the same thing over and over for days."

"Maybe that's all he'll have to say when you get there," Joe cautioned. "I don't want you to be upset if he can't tell you everything you want to hear."

He reached over and squeezed her hand.

"Thanks, Joe," she said softly. "I need to see him again regardless of what happens. I want to see everybody in Cajun Corners! I want to go home!"

Joe stopped squeezing her hand, but he didn't let go for a while. He was pleased that she didn't pull away.

"Why don't you try to sleep some while I'm driving?" he suggested. "You may be up with Great Pa tonight."

"I don't know if I can," she said.

"Come on," he said. "Put your head on my shoulder and close your eyes."

Kana obeyed. As she drifted off to sleep, she felt like she was already home.

While Kana slept, Joe let go of her hand and put both

hands on the steering wheel again. He glanced at her. She was so innocent and vulnerable. He thought of ways he could protect her. Doug had told him on the phone that the guards Jim Granger had posted were still there, but Fetney Lou and Oscoe would help him keep Kana from seeing them. He had called for backup, but he would have to hide his men in the swamp away from the fields. Now there was nothing else he could do until they got to Silver Mist.

Chapter Fourteen

Sheila had gone straight to bed when she arrived at the hotel from the airport.

Now, still exhausted and groggy from an interrupted sleep, she tried to ignore the insistent ringing of the phone. The throbbing in her head finally forced her to answer.

Jim Granger's voice came to her ear, loud and angry!

"Just what do you think you're doing?" he shouted.

"Sleeping until you called!" snapped Sheila. "What do you want at this hour?"

"Look, Sheila, I'm not in the mood for any of your lip!" he continued. "That little stunt you pulled last night to get Kana angry with me worked. When I called her this morning, she broke our engagement. I gave her a little time to cool off and called back, but the maid said she wasn't there. She'd found a letter from Doug and Nicole telling her that the old man's been asking for her. She left for Silver Mist with Joe Tarwater!"

"Joe Tarwater?" said Sheila. "I don't understand."

"Then you'd better listen up," he said, his voice still loud. "Joe Tarwater brought a tape of William's songs to Nat's office yesterday. He said he wanted to warn you to straighten things out. He wanted to show you proof that he's on to you."

"Oh, no!" said Sheila.

"It gets worse," Jim informed her, lowering his voice now that he had her attention. "Kana came in while he was there. She thought he'd brought his own songs for you to hear, so she took the tape to give to you. I managed to get it away from her this morning before she had a chance to listen to it. She couldn't have heard much at Nat's office."

"Oh, dear," said Sheila, trying to take in all he was telling her.

"You told me you had everything under control, Sheila!" Jim continued. "But I think you've tried to double cross me. Now, if this Joe Tarwater gets in my way, you will see what real trouble is!"

Sheila had never heard Jim's voice so threatening before.

"I don't know how Joe Tarwater found out," said Sheila, "but Kana and I had nothing to do with it! Why can't you move your operation away from Silver Mist and leave us alone?"

"It's too late for that," Jim answered. "Besides, I like Silver Mist. Now you take care of Kana and I'll take care of Joe Tarwater."

"Like you took care of William?" accused Sheila.

Jim ignored her question.

"You've screwed up everything, Sheila," he said. "Now you are going to help me straighten it out."

Sheila cringed at the menacing tone in his voice. She tried to sound calm when she spoke again.

"What do you mean?" she asked.

"I'm going to Silver Mist and try to persuade Kana that she can't live without me. You are going to do your shows in Vegas and join me at Cajun Corners so you can help convince her. You'd better do a good job of it, Sheila, unless you want to spend the rest of your life rotting away in that swamp!"

"Do I have a choice?" asked Sheila.

"No!" he answered, and hung up without waiting for her reply.

Sheila cradled the phone in her hand and cried. Jim Granger was wrong. Of course, she had a choice! She wasn't at all sure that she had the courage to make it, though. She had worked so hard to get what she had, and she didn't know if she would have the strength to give it up. She prayed to have the courage to do the right thing when the time came.

She had always felt alone until she became immersed in her music. Her mother had done the best could, but she couldn't change the fact that Sheila was not like the other kids in the schools in Cajun Corners. They had fathers and Sheila didn't! That made her an outcast. She had asked her mother about her father once, but she had said he was not worth discussing. Sheila had seen the hurt in her mother's eyes, so she never asked her again.

She had asked Oscoe, though. He told her he had only seen him once. He had come from the outside world and he had taken Fetney Lou back there with him. But only Fetney Lou had returned. He had been a doctor, but he'd only brought pain!

She could see that Oscoe had felt the pain, too, so she never mentioned him again.

When she had gotten rich, she had thought of trying to find him. She hired a detective, who learned that her father had been married when he got Fetney Lou pregnant. She let the matter drop. There was no use hurting his family. She had done all right without him growing up. She didn't need him now. Oscoe was the one who had been there for her and Fetney Lou through the years. He was the only father that mattered.

Sheila had often wondered why Fetney Lou and Oscoe had never married. She heard enough gossip at school to know it was a subject she'd better not approach. She wished they could have been a family. Her happiest memories were of the nights when Oscoe brought fish for supper, or Fetney Lou asked him over for her special gumbo.

After supper when the dishes were done, Oscoe and Fetney Lou would sit on the porch and talk quietly. Sheila would listen to songs on the old radio that popped and cracked with static. She would dream of places far away from Cajun Corners, dreams that Fetney Lou said were foolish and impossible.

But the dreams had come true. And they had been wonderful until Jim Granger came along and turned them into a nightmare. Realizing the danger that surrounded Kana had been a wakeup call. To expose Jim was to expose herself, but she had to save Kana at all costs!

Chapter Fifteen

The old man opened his eyes and looked around. He had no idea of what time it was. He could see Nicole moving about the room dusting. Why was she here in his room? He moved his lips to speak, but no sound came.

In his mind, he could see the old hollow cypress tree. Thoughts and images came so fast, he couldn't sort them. He needed to get them out. He needed to tell someone about that day. He had lived it over and over for four years. Maybe he could stop if he could only tell somebody! He had often heard voices far away, but he had been trapped in a gray, timeless world. He began to live it again.

It had been warm, so he had gone for a walk. He hadn't been to the back fields for weeks, so he headed in that direction. The path led through the edge of the swamp, so he took it, eager for the shade.

As he came near to the old cypress tree, he heard voices. It would be pleasant to have company on his walk. He recognized William's voice, but he wasn't sure about the other. At first, he thought maybe it was Oscoe, but he knew it wasn't when the voices suddenly turned angry. He hurried closer and saw William and his new attorney, Jim Granger, in an obvious confrontation. He couldn't hear what they were arguing about, but Granger's tone was ugly. He caught snatches of the conversation.

"Get out of the back fields!" William was saying.

Jim Granger laughed harshly.

"Destroy the crops or I will!" William ordered.

"If you destroy my crops, I'll look up that pretty little daughter of yours," Jim threatened.

"Over my dead body!" said William.

Their voices continued, tense and low. Great Pa had moved up undetected and heard everything. Oh, God! It hurt too much to remember alone! He wanted to tell someone!

Great Pa opened his mouth again and concentrated all his efforts on speaking.

"Kana," he said. "Mari–"

Nicole dropped her dusting rag and rushed to his bed. She took his hand and squeezed it.

"Kana's coming," she said. "She's on her way right now. Joe Tarwater is driving her down, and they'll be here very soon. Hold on, Great Pa!"

The old man thought how nice that would be. Joe Tarwater was a good man. He'd get Kana here safely. He could talk to Kana. She would understand. It wouldn't be long now. He closed his eyes, and this time, his sleep was peaceful.

Chapter Sixteen

Kana woke up when Joe took the exit from the interstate to the two-lane highway that wound into the swamp. Joe smiled at her, but kept silent, giving his attention to his driving. Kana was content to watch the familiar scenery roll by.

"Why didn't you wake me, Joe?" she asked, rubbing her eyes.

"You looked exhausted," he said. "Besides I'm used to driving alone. Are you feeling better?"

"I've been feeling better ever since I left Nashville," Kana said, truthfully.

After the third sharp curve, they came upon the old, weatherbeaten sign announcing that Cajun Corners was twelve miles ahead.

"It won't be long now," Joe commented.

"No, it won't," said Kana, excited by the prospect of being at Silver Mist again, but a little disappointed with herself for sleeping through so much of this time she had alone with Joe. She had awakened only when they stopped to eat. She had even ordered coffee to keep her awake, but it hadn't worked. Back on the road, she had fallen asleep again.

It was dark now. The moon was up, glowing softly in

patches of water near the road. Gnarled old stumps twisted up from inky pools, like creatures in a science fiction movie. Low handing branches scraped against the car top, causing Kana to shudder. She hadn't remembered how spooky it could be here after sundown. She was grateful she had not come alone. Without thinking, she slid a little closer to Joe.

They were driving along the river now, and Kana could see the silhouette of Oscoe's house boat. Great Pa had taken her there often to visit. She could picture every inch of it. The shingles were black with age, and a stovepipe stuck out of the roof near the back. The furnishings were simple and solid like Oscoe himself. She sometimes wondered why he lived like that. He was a writer and his books and drawings sold well.

She had asked him once. He had smiled and said this was everything he needed.

The road turned away from the river, and Kana watched the countryside flash by.

They were very near Silver Mist now. How sweet it was to be coming home!

The back fields were beyond the trees to her right. Kana was looking in that direction when a cloud blocked the moon. Through the darkness, she saw lights flickering in the distance.

"Look, Joe!" she exclaimed. "There are lights in the back fields. Who could be back there?"

"Must be the lights in town," said Joe.

"No!" said Kana. "The town is not that way! Geez! I haven't lost my sense of direction since I've been gone. I was looking toward the back fields, and I'm certain I saw lights moving back there!"

"I didn't see anything," said Joe.

"Well, I did!" Kana insisted. "Something's going on."

"What could possibly be back there?" asked Joe. "You know there are no roads in the back fields."

"I don't know," said Kana, with determination, "but you can bet I'll find out in the morning!"

"Maybe it was foxfire," said Joe. "It gives off light."

"And maybe it was Martians," said Kana, annoyed with him for not taking her seriously.

Joe realized he hadn't handled her discovery of the lights very well.

"I'm sorry, Kana," he apologized. "I believe you. I don't want you worrying about anything while you are here with Great Pa. I'll go out and check myself as soon as I get you to Silver Mist. Will that make you feel better?"

Kana was feeling a little silly now about her outburst. She didn't want Joe to go way back there after this long drive.

"I'm sorry, too," she said. "You don't need to check. It's probably some hunters on their way home. Whatever it is, it can wait until morning."

"I'll check it then personally, just in case it's Martians," Joe teased. "I would feel awful if they encountered you in the mood you're in now. It would be bad public relations."

Kana laughed.

"Are we still friends?" he asked.

"Still friends," she laughed again.

They rode on in easy silence. Kana said nothing else about the lights, but he knew she wasn't satisfied yet about what she had seen. He hoped she wouldn't get too curious.

He would have to make sure she didn't go off on her own. Martians would be more desirable to deal with than those goons of Granger's guarding the back fields. He would have to work fast to make sure Kana had no close encounters with them!

Chapter Seventeen

The *krrummp* of bullfrogs sounded like a chorus on the mossy riverbank. Other night creatures joined in unseen, with rustlings and slitherings. The bayou swamp was full of wildlife – alligators, muskrats, nutria, mink, raccoons, rabbits, skunks, wildcats, squirrels, white-tailed deer, and snakes! And there were birds of all sizes and colors.

Oscoe had an endless supply of things to sketch and write about. He carefully studied all of it.

Fetney Lou knew all the wildlife. From where she stood on her short night walk, she could see the faint light in Oscoe's window. Her heart still swelled with love when she thought of him. *Lord, why did I do such a foolish thing and lose him?*

Familiar scents came to her on the gentle bayou breeze. Then tonight, like an omen, she got a whiff of moldy, decaying vegetation along with sweet mimosa and honeysuckle. She loved this place and hated what was happening now. The lights moving in the back fields angered her. Outsiders always angered her now. If not for an outsider, she might have married Oscoe.

She thought of Sheila's marriage to William. He had been a good man. He had tried to drive the vermin out, but it had cost him his life. Sheila had brought this on them all when she had chosen the outside world. Then she had persuaded William to take Kana with them on a European tour, even though she kept them in the background. It was during William's absence that Jim Granger and his hoods had managed to get a hold on Silver Mist. When they returned, William had discovered the crops growing in the back fields. He couldn't believe he was seeing marijuana plants, coca bushes, and opium poppies on his plantation! Great Pa had turned everything over to Jim Granger, never suspecting the crops were illegal. Great Pa had been glad to be relieved of responsibility so he could go off fishing! William didn't want Great Pa to blame himself, so he went alone to confront Granger.

William was shocked when Jim informed him that Sheila knew about the whole operation. He couldn't believe she would knowingly be a party to such a thing. Since she was on the road again, he couldn't ask her for an explanation. Jim had promised William proof. They were to meet that fatal morning by the old hollow cypress.

Jim had called Sheila to come to Cajun Corners secretly as his proof. She hadn't arrived when the two met at the cypress, but she had flown in and was on her way there through the swamp. She had to make William understand that she had been blackmailed into accepting Granger's plan.

Nobody knew now what happened under the tree that day except the old man and the killer. Until a few days ago, the old man had been silenced by the stroke. Fetney Lou often wondered who could have been in the swamp that day. *Who would have wanted William dead?*

As Fetney Lou started back home from her walk, she saw

car lights come down the road and stop at Silver Mist. That would be Joe and Kana. Doug had told her and Oscoe they were coming. She hoped they were doing the right thing in letting Kana see Great Pa! Now that she was here, it would be impossible to keep her away from him.

They would have to be on guard to keep Kana safe until they knew the identity of the killer. If the killer had a chance to get to Great Pa to silence him forever, Kana could very well be killed in the process. She would have to be silenced, too, if she knew.

Doug's idea to try to frighten Kana away would be worth a try. That part would be up to her and Oscoe. She didn't think that Kana would be frightened by bayou magic, but she had no other ideas. She and Oscoe had prepared the magic. They were ready.

As Fetney Lou reached her front door, the swamp sounds stopped abruptly. The night breeze suddenly turned cold. She drew her tattered shawl tighter around her bony shoulders and stepped inside. She had no doubt that death was near. She just wasn't sure who would be its victim.

Chapter Eighteen

As Joe turned onto the long, winding drive in front of Silver Mist, lights moved along the boundaries of the back fields.

"Look!" said Kana. "There are those lights again! Now don't tell me you didn't see them this time, Joe Tarwater!"

There was no denying it this time. The lights were gone now, but they had been directly in his line of vision. They had reached the house, so Joe turned off the ignition before he spoke. He had to think fast to come up with an explanation that would satisfy Kana.

"I'd hoped I wouldn't have to tell you this, Kana," Joe lied, "but we've had some trouble with poachers lately. Folks are afraid there will be trouble before we get rid of them."

"Well, why didn't you tell me that?" she asked.

"I told you I didn't want anything worrying you on your visit with Great Pa," said Joe, speaking the truth this time. "This could be a dangerous situation, so I want you to promise me that you will stay close to the house until I get this settled."

"Okay, I promise," said Kana, "but I don't see anything so dangerous about a few poachers."

"I wouldn't want you caught in the crossfire," said Joe.

"Crossfire?" she asked. "Is there going to be shooting?"

"I hope not," he said, "but you never know when a situation can turn ugly."

"Is there anything I can do?" asked Kana.

"Just let me handle it," said Joe. "It's part of my job. Now let's go inside and see your grandfather."

"Okay," agreed Kana, "but I have a feeling there's something you're not telling me, Joe Tarwater!"

As he helped her out of the car, the porch light came on. Joe was spared having to answer because Doug and Nicole came running to greet them.

"I can't wait to see Great Pa," said Kana, between the smiles and hugs. "Is he awake?"

"Not right now," said Doug. "Let's get you settled in and then we'll see if he wakes up."

"Then I leave you in good hands," said Joe.

"Aren't you coming in?" she asked.

"Not now," said Joe. "I need a word with Doug."

"Joe, thank you for driving me here!" said Kana. "Will I see you tomorrow?"

"You couldn't keep me away," he told her.

"Come on inside with me," Nicole said, taking her arm and guiding her up the walk. "Doug can bring your luggage."

From the door, Kana could see the two men talking with their heads bent close before Joe got in his car and pulled away. It looked very secretive to Kana, but she couldn't imagine what secrets those two could have.

Doug came inside right behind Nicole and Kana. He carried Kana's bags to her old room. As they passed Great Pa's door, they stopped and looked inside. The old man was sleeping peacefully, but tears came to Kana's eyes when she saw how frail he had become.

"You have time for a good hot bath," said Nicole. "I'll let you know when he wakes up."

It was after her bath as she stood by her open window that she realized nobody had asked anything about Sheila. Joe must have told Doug all that had happened. She took a deep breath of fresh air and saw the lights again briefly. She wondered if Joe had gone to the back fields when he left. She couldn't help but feel that there was something not quite right about the story he'd told her about poachers. They had gotten rid of poachers in Cajun Corners before without problems. *Why was Joe in on it? Why didn't the local sheriff just run them off?*

There was a knock on the door. Nicole came in with some tea.

"He's not awake yet," she said to Kana. "Drink this. It will help you rest, too."

Nicole slipped quietly out the door and Kana sipped her tea. She left the window and slid under the covers on her bed. Maybe Joe would have good news in the morning.

As she drifted off to sleep, she heard a faint moan down the hall. It must be Great Pa waking up. She wanted to go see, but her eyelids were too heavy. She slept and dreamed of strange sounds and footsteps.

Chapter Nineteen

Kana slept until almost ten o'clock the next morning. Maybe it was the tea. She had meant to take a walk early, see the sunrise, and watch the bayou come alive with the pelicans, wood ducks, herons and egrets. It was obviously too late for that now.

She jumped out of bed to dress, but the damp morning air sent her scurrying to close the window. As she looked out, she was surprised to see two cars parked in the drive. One was Joe Tarwater's and the other was Dr. Blanton's. She was expecting Joe, but she knew Dr. Blanton wouldn't be here unless it was to see Great Pa!

Maybe the doctor comes by to check on him every day she thought, trying to control her fear as she threw on her clothes and ran down the hall.

Doug, Nicole, and Joe were standing grim-faced outside of Great Pa's closed door.

"What's wrong?" she cried. "Has something happened to Great Pa?"

Joe hurried to her and put his arms around her.

"Take it easy," he said.

"What is Dr. Blanton doing here?" Kana questioned. "Tell me what's wrong."

"Come downstairs and have some coffee with me," he said, " and I'll tell you everything we know."

"I hope so!" said Kana, allowing Joe to lead her down the stairs and seat her at the table. "Everybody has been keeping secrets from me lately and I don't like it! I'm not a child!"

"So I've noticed," smiled Joe, handing her a steaming cup of coffee. "You drink and I'll talk."

"What happened?" Kana asked again, sipping the coffee and beginning to calm down a bit.

"There was an intruder last night," Joe explained in a low voice. "Someone got into your grandfather's room and tried to smother him."

"Oh, my God!" cried Kana. "Is he all right?"

"We think so," said Joe. "The doctor is with him now, so we'll have to wait and see."

Kana began to sob, and Joe came and knelt beside her and held her while she cried.

"I knew I should have gone in there last night," said Kana. "Maybe this wouldn't have happened if I had stayed with him."

"Kana, I didn't want you in there alone," said Joe. "In fact, I don't want you going anywhere alone until we find out who the intruder was. Honey, the killer would come after you, too, if he thought Great Pa had revealed his identity to you."

"Oh, Joe, this means the killer is someone we know, right?" she asked.

"Most likely," said Joe.

Tears came again, and Joe handed her a napkin.

"Here, dry your eyes," he told her. "Let's go up and see if the doctor has finished his examination."

Joe kept his arm around her as they climbed the stairs. She felt comforted by the strength of him.

"I can't believe this!" she said to Nicole and Doug, who were still waiting outside the door.

"I can't either," said Doug. "I was with him, Kana, but I dozed off in my chair, I woke up when I heard him moan, and all I could see was a hooded figure bending over him. I yelled and jumped up, and whoever it was ran into the hall. I ran to check on Great Pa, so he got a head start. By the time I saw that Great Pa was breathing, the intruder was gone. Nicole called Joe and Dr. Blanton."

"Why didn't you call the sheriff?" Kana wanted to know.

"Joe was closer," said Nicole. "He was right next door."

"There is something going on here that you all are not telling me," said Kana. "I want to know what it is!"

Doug looked at Joe. Joe took a deep breath and looked at Kana.

"Kana, I have accepted a temporary job as a special investigator for the state," he said. "Some things are going on around here that need to be handled by someone familiar with the area."

"What things?" asked Kana. "Poachers?"

"No," said Joe. "I lied about that. I'm sorry. It was all I could think of. I can't tell you everything yet. You'll have to trust me. Can you do that?"

"After you just admitted you lied about the poachers?" asked Kana.

Joe started to answer, but the door opened and Dr. Blanton came out of Great Pa's room.

"How is he?" asked Nicole.

"He's stable now," said the doctor, "but he's had a bad shock. He must have complete rest."

"Can't I please see him for just a minute?" pleaded Kana. "I want to let him know I'm here."

"Not now, Kana," Dr. Blanton told her. "It might excite him too much. I'll be back to check on him this afternoon. We'll talk about it then. Meanwhile, let him sleep."

"I'll walk you to your car," said Joe, giving Kana a quick hug before he let her go. "I have a couple of questions that will take just a minute."

"Try not to worry," said Dr. Blanton, nodding goodbye.

Kana, Doug, and Nicole stood in the hallway, not knowing exactly what to do next. Doug was the first to speak.

"Kana, you know I would never let anyone hurt Great Pa if I could help it."

"I know that, Doug," she answered. "I'm not blaming you and Nicole. I simply can't understand why anyone would want to harm such a gentle, sweet old man!"

"Neither do I," said Nicole. "But we'll find out!"

"I'm going to sleep today," said Doug, "so I won't doze off tonight. I'll make sure that nobody gets to him again!"

"Who could be trying to kill him?" asked Kana. "I know there's something going on that I should know!"

"What do you mean?" asked Nicole quickly.

"Well, those lights I saw last night for one thing," said Kana. "Joe told me it was poachers, but he just admitted that he lied!"

"Must you always be so nosey?" asked Joe, coming back up the stairs.

"I do if I am going to find out what's going on!" she retorted.

"I'll tell you what's going on," he said lightly. "Doug is going to get some sleep and Nicole is going to sit with Great Pa. I am going to take you away for a while so they can do what they need to do!"

Joe took her arm and steered her down the stairs and out the front door.

"Wait!" she protested. "Where are you taking me?"

"You'll see," he said. "Trust me."

Joe's hand firmly directed her down the walk to his car. He opened the door and practically stuffed her in. She considered getting out as he walked around to get in, but she had to admit that this was exciting.

Joe watched the road silently as he drove toward Cajun Corners. Kana kept quiet, too, and looked at the little town as they drove through. There weren't many changes since she had been here four years ago. There was still one main street, but a traffic light had been added. Nobody seemed to be stirring.

Outside of town, Joe turned off onto the narrow road that led to the swamp.

From the corner of her eye, Kana could see the stubborn set of Joe's jaw. She ventured to speak anyway.

"Would you mind telling me where we're going?"

"Fishing," he said.

"Fishing!" she repeated incredulously. "At a time like this?"

"It's one of the best ways to get rid of stress," he said. "At least one of the best ways that can involve you right now!"

Kana felt herself blushing at the intimate way he looked at her. She was glad they had reached the riverbank so she could get some fresh air! She breathed deeply as he walked around the car.

"What will we fish with?" she said. "I have no gear!"

Joe raised the trunk lid and removed two fishing rods. Carrying both, he guided Kana to small boat with an outboard motor.

"I always carry extra equipment in my car," he said. "Step in carefully."

She hesitated as he placed the rods in the boat.

"You know there are laws against kidnapping in this state, even for special agents, don't you?" grinned Kana.

Joe gripped her shoulders and spun her around facing him. The action was so unexpected that it threw Kana forward against him. His arms held her there.

"Kana," he said softly, his lips brushing hers gently, "sometimes you ask too many questions!"

Her arms went up around his neck as his lips touched hers again, the gentleness replaced with urgency this time. Lights exploded in Kana's head like a hundred suns breaking through dense morning fog. For the moment, these were the only lights Kana cared about.

Chapter Twenty

Sheila's last show had gone well. She was always on a natural high after a good performance, and she wasn't down yet after this one. She could still hear the music and the cheering of the fans.

The sound of the phone intruded rudely.

Sheila answered and Jim Granger began speaking without a hello.

"I'm staying at the Cajun Corners Motel," he said. "Nobody knows I'm here, but I had a close call at Silver Mist last night. I almost had the old man silenced permanently, but the bodyguard woke up."

"What?" Sheila asked, the shock showing in her voice. "I don't believe that even *you* could do such a horrible thing!" His words had brought her down fast. She had never imagined he would go this far.

"Get down here fast," he ordered. "You've got work to do!"

"I'll be there all right," said Sheila, with a new tone in her voice that he didn't notice.

"Don't go straight to the main house," he instructed. "Check with me first. Things are moving pretty fast. The old man may still die from the shock I gave him, but I've got to plan my next move in case he doesn't."

"Where shall I meet you?" asked Sheila.

"By the old cypress tree near the old woman's cabin," he said.

"Fine," she said. *How fitting*, she thought!

"When will you leave?" he asked.

"Tonight," she told him. "I'll stay with Fetney Lou."

"Then I'll see you in the morning about ten," he said.

"Right," she answered.

"And, Sheila, " he added " if you cross me, your daughter is as good as dead!"

"I'll do what I have to do," said Sheila quietly.

"See that you do!" he threatened, and abruptly ended the call.

Sheila sat gathering her strength. She had always seen herself as weak until now. She had depended on others for support, but now they were gone.

"I'll do what I have to do," she said again.

Fetney Lou and Oscoe would probably help her. Oscoe's influence had mellowed her mother somewhat toward her. Doug and Nicole would help for the sake of Great Pa and Kana. Maybe Joe Tarwater might be of some assistance, too. She did not want to put any of them in danger, though. Mostly, it would be up to her to put things right.

She would have to go to Cajun Corners and meet Jim, but if she hurried she still had time to go by her studio in Nashville and get the last song she'd cut. It was the first song she had written by herself, and she was proud of it. She wanted to get copies for Kana and Fetney Lou. It would be her way of bringing them together at last.

When her plane touched down in Nashville, she did what she needed to do there.

Airborne again, she wrote a hasty dedication for the CD insert. She copied it by hand on the special copies for Kana and Fetney Lou. Then she wrote a long letter and addressed it to Joe Tarwater. She dropped it in the mail slot at the airport when The Snowy Heron touched down in Louisiana. Then she headed for the first place she had called home.

She felt a great sense of relief now. Somebody would know the truth. She had never intended to get mixed up in anything like murder. She had never wanted to hurt anyone at all. Joe Tarwater would know what to do with the information she had sent him. She had to draw the line somewhere, even though it would probably mean the end the line for her.

Chapter Twenty-one

Joe cut the motor and kept the boat in shallow water. The next two hours went fine. Beyond a brief statement that the lights were government business that he couldn't discuss, Joe told Kana nothing.

"Trust me," he kept saying.

Kana found it hard to trust anyone, but there was no reason not to trust Joe. In any case, she had no choice. She tried to put all the bad things out of her mind, but she found herself thinking more and more about last night. The moan and footsteps that had been part of her dream must have been real.

"Isn't it time for Dr. Blanton to check Great Pa?" she finally asked.

Joe glanced at his watch.

"Yes," he said. "I'll take you back."

"Good," said Kana. "I'm hungry!"

"Have you calmed down, now?" he asked.

Kana smiled and nodded.

"Thanks for bringing me out here, Joe," she said. "I probably would have upset the whole household if I had stayed at Silver Mist!"

"I was glad to sacrifice my morning for the sake of peace,"

laughed Joe. "You know how I hate fishing!"

Both were laughing as they drove away. They stopped only for a quick lunch.

When they arrived at Silver Mist, Dr. Blanton had just finished his examination of Great Pa. He nodded when he saw Kana outside her grandfather's door and motioned for her to come in.

Kana ran to the bed and took the old man's hand. How different it was now than when they had walked among the trees in the swamp! It seemed like only yesterday that they had taken those walks together. A wave of anger flooded through her as she thought of anyone wanting to hurt him. She squeezed his hand and he opened his eyes. They were alert and clear.

"Great Pa," she said softly, "it's me – Kana."

His eyes sparkled with recognition, but he did not speak.

"I love you," said Kana. "We all love you. We are going to take care of you, so you'll be fine. Do you feel like talking?"

She felt a slight pressure from his hand, but his eyes closed.

"He's still weak," said Dr. Blanton. "Let him rest now. You may come back later. I'll check again in the morning."

"Thank you, doctor," said Kana.

Joe left right after Dr. Blanton, and Kana helped Nicole prepare supper. They ate mostly in silence.

After supper, Doug began preparations to stand guard with Great Pa, and Kana went up to her room. She soaked in a hot bath and remembered the feel of Joe Tarwater's lips. He hadn't kissed her again, though she had wanted him to. She lay in bed and tried to read, but she kept seeing Joe's face. *What secret case could he be working on here in Cajun Corners? Where was he now? Was he outside somewhere watching the house, making sure she and Great Pa were safe? But from what or whom?*

The night sounds were soothing, but she knew she couldn't sleep yet. She needed to look at the stars. As she crossed to the window, she heard a muffled thud outside. She stood there motionless, glad that she had turned out the light.

As she watched, a figure stepped out from the veranda below and looked up at the second floor windows. She couldn't be sure it was a man, but it seemed too tall for a woman. A dark coat and hood concealed the intruder's identity.

The killer! thought Kana, her stomach tight with fear. *Oh, God! Maybe he's after Great Pa again!*

She was about to run screaming for Doug, when she saw him come outside.

Lights bobbed in from the swamp, and several figures moved shadow-like among the trees. Doug and the hooded figure on the veranda crossed the lawn to meet them. She noticed something familiar about the figure with Doug. He walked the same way Jim Granger walked! But that was impossible! Jim was in Vegas with Sheila.

Kana watched as the men stood talking. She couldn't hear a sound. She felt like she was watching a silent movie! The talking stopped and the lights bobbed back into the swamp, and the hooded figure followed them. Doug came back into the house. Kana heard him walk softly up the stairs to Great Pa's room and close the door.

Kana's first impulse was to run to Great Pa's room and confront Doug, but she was distracted by a movement near the trees. She was startled to see a bent figure dart to the veranda and place something by the back door. Then it left as silently and swiftly as it come.

Maybe that was Fetney Lou. The strange old woman had often given Kana gifts. *Maybe she had left a welcoming bouquet!*

Even though she was curious, Kana could not gather the courage to go down and see. Instead, she forced herself to leave the window and go back to bed. For the first time, she felt in danger in Silver Mist! *What was going on? Who was involved? Who could she trust?* It was almost morning when she finally fell asleep.

Chapter Twenty-two

Sheila took the back roads to Cajun Corners to avoid being seen. She stopped by Oscoe's houseboat and woke him before going to her mother's cabin. He brewed a pot of strong coffee and listened to her story without judgment.

"Do you want me to walk you to Fetney Lou's?" he asked.

"No," she said. "But come over later if you can."

"I will," he promised.

She thanked him and made her way through the swamp to the cabin. Dawn was breaking as she reached the door and knocked.

"It's open!" called Fetney Lou.

Sheila opened the door and stepped into the warm, cozy room.

"Hello, Mother," she said.

"So you've come back again," said the old woman without emotion.

"Yes," said Sheila, "but I don't have much time. Kana's in danger. Will you help me help her?"

"For the girl's sake, I'll do what I can," Fetney Lou answered.

The door opened and the two women turned to see Oscoe standing there.

"I left the flowers from the mangrove tree by the back door," he said, as if he had been part of the conversation all along.

"Kana is too practical to be frightened away from Silver Mist by witches' signs," said Sheila. "That will never keep her from going to the back fields if she sets her head."

"It's worth a try," said Fetney Lou.

"I'd try anything to keep Kana safe," said Sheila.

Fetney Lou looked at her daughter in a new light. *Was it possible that the spoiled, successful superstar was finally thinking of someone other than herself?* She looked closer and saw the determination in Sheila's eyes. It was true. Sheila had certainly changed!

"I am glad to hear you say that," said Fetney Lou. "For a while, I wondered!"

"Having her with me on the road made me realize how precious she is to me," said Sheila. "I never realized I was putting her in such danger."

"When I was at the house, I saw Jim Granger sneaking away," said Oscoe.

"What was he doing there?" asked Sheila, frightened that he might have attacked Great Pa again.

"I couldn't be sure," said Oscoe. "I couldn't hear much of what was said, but it sounded like he'd been spotted in town and was trying to set up some kind of cover story in case Kana heard. His guards were there, too, but Doug put all of them out fast."

"Did Kana see them?" asked Sheila.

"I don't think so," said Oscoe. "I think she was already asleep. I didn't see a light in her room when I left the warning and headed home."

"What about Great Pa?" asked Sheila.

" A little better maybe," said Oscoe. "Somebody's with him to protect him day and night."

"I wish that were true of Kana," said Sheila.

"Joe will take care of her," said Oscoe. "He took her fishing yesterday. He'll take her somewhere today."

Sheila smiled at the thought of them together. Joe was a good man.

"Good," she said. "That will give me time to get things settled. I'm meeting Jim by the cypress at ten this morning."

"Then you've got time for breakfast," said Fetney Lou.

She fried ham, eggs, and made biscuits, and the three of them ate. For that time, Sheila was a child again with the people she loved. She watched the sun climb over the trees.

"It's time I was on my way," she said.

She bent and kissed her mother's cheek, and the old woman held her daughter's face tenderly in her hands. She smiled and watched as Sheila vanished among the trees like she did when she was a carefree little girl. Oscoe sat with her in silence.

Chapter Twenty-three

The hooded figure had given Kana bad dreams. She woke early, glad that the dream shadows had not been real. She took a quick shower and pulled on jeans and a blue top. She was on her way to breakfast when she heard an ear-splitting scream!

Kana entered the kitchen just in time to see Doug and Nicole comforting the cook.

"What's wrong?" asked Kana, alarmed.

"This!" said the cook. Her voice shook as she pointed to the creamy white bouquet by the door.

"They're just flowers," said Kana.

"Nine flowers!" said the cook. "A witch's curse!"

"It's all right," said Nicole.

Doug's face was troubled, but he remained silent.

Kana stepped to the door for a closer look.

"It's no curse," she told the poor trembling woman. "It's probably for me. Fetney Lou used to leave me things like this when I lived here. I saw someone put it here after your guest left last night, Doug."

"M-my guest?" stammered Doug, surprised by the sudden revelation that Kana had seen him and the others last night.

"I thought I heard a prowler," said Kana. "I was worried about Great Pa and started to call you, but I saw you come out and talk to the man."

Doug looked uncomfortable.

"That was one of Joe's men that he sent to check on things," said Doug.

'Do guards wear dark hooded coats, now?" asked Kana.

Nicole took Doug's arm. He ignored the remark.

"I saw the lights again," said Kana. "There was more than one man out there last night."

"Doug," said Nicole, "don't you–"

Doug cut her off with a stern look.

"Kana, I told you that Joe posted some guards around because of what happened to Great Pa," Doug said.

"Why were there so many?" asked Kana.

Doug was spared having to explain further by Joe Tarwater's voice announcing his arrival.

"Hey!" he called. "Anybody home? Where is everybody?"

"Out here!" Doug yelled back.

Joe came into the kitchen and saw the four of them, standing near the back door looking out.

"Did I miss something?" he asked, raising his eyebrows.

"It's a witch's curse," sobbed the cook, running from the room. Nicole hurried after her.

Kana looked from Doug to Joe Tarwater, but she said nothing. She picked up an undercurrent between the two men.

"What's going on here?" asked Joe. "Don't I even get a 'good morning,' Kana?"

"Good morning, Joe," she said sweetly.

"Kana's a little upset with us," Doug said to Joe. "She saw

your guards near the house with their lights last night. Now she thinks we had mysterious visitors. She saw me go out and talk to them, so she has a lot of questions. I told her you sent them to check on Great Pa, and that I gave them a report and sent them on their way. Then she saw someone put this here."

You filled him in, Doug, Kana thought, *but you didn't do it too smoothly. You are not fooling me.*

Doug pointed to the white flowers.

"I'm sorry you were frightened, Kana," said Joe.

"I wasn't frightened by these," said Kana. "Fetney Lou used to bring me these when I lived at Silver Mist with father. What frightens me is that I am being kept in the dark about what is really going on here. You two must take me for a fool! I do not appreciate being lied to!"

"I don't know what you're talking about,' said Doug.

"You have an overactive imagination, Lady," said Joe. The tone indicated that she would get no more information or argument from him on the subject. "Now how about a ride in the country to cool off?"

Kana hated being treated like a child, but if they wanted to play games, she'd go along. She'd make them think she was playing by their rules, but she would do some investigating on her own. She could sneak out tonight and check the back fields herself.

She'd let them think she was going along with their stories.

"You know, Joe?" she said reaching for his hand, "I think a ride in the country would be nice."

Chapter Twenty-four

"You certainly are quiet," Joe remarked, as they drove toward Cajun Corners. "Are you okay?"

"I never got my morning coffee," said Kana.

"We can fix that," said Joe. "The diner is coming up right around the bend. It should be open by now."

"Thank you," said Kana. "I haven't been there for quite a while!"

Clem Sanders was unlocking the door to his store next to the diner when they pulled in.

"What you know, you?" he called.

The old Cajun dialect sounded like sweet music to Kana's ears. She used to come here with Great Pa and listen to all the conversations. If anyone would know what was going on in Cajun Corners, Clem would!

"Come have some coffee with us, Clem," she called. "I want to hear about everything that has happened since I've been away."

Kana pretended not to see Joe scowling, and Clem didn't notice at all. He hurried to join them as they entered the diner.

The place wasn't crowded, so they selected a booth in the back where they could talk. Clem was delighted to have an audience. They ordered coffee and doughnuts and chatted about the old times and all the people they knew. Joe began to relax and Kana began to give up on gleaning any information about current happenings from Clem, when he suddenly looked at her and threw up his hands.

"I just remembered, yes," he said. "A man was in my store late yesterday asking all about our town. He had a license plate from Tennessee. Asked about you and Sheila, yes!"

"Really?" asked Kana, innocently. "What did he look like?"

She listened while he described Jim Granger perfectly.

"You know this man?" asked Clem.

"Maybe," said Kana.

"Probably one of Sheila's fans," said Joe.

"Probably," Kana agreed

"I got to go open my store now," said Clem. "When Sheila comes to Cajun Corners, tell her to come say hello."

"I will," promised Kana.

Joe had listened quietly until Clem mentioned the stranger. Kana noticed that he had tried to interrupt, but had been unable to stop Clem from continuing. He looked relieved when Clem announced that he had to go.

Things were beginning to click now. The hooded figure at Silver Mist had walked like Jim Granger. Now Clem had described a stranger in town that sounded like him, too.

It didn't make sense to her that he'd be here, but she had to know. She slipped her hand in her purse and pulled out her wallet. As Clem stood up to leave, Kana quietly handed him a picture.

"Is this the man?" she asked.

Clem looked at the picture.

"Yes!" he said, surprised. "That's the man! So you know

him after all?"

"Not as well as I thought," said Kana. "I didn't think I'd be seeing him here in Cajun Corners."

"I hope I did right in telling," said Clem. "Did I ruin a surprise?"

"Not at all, Clem," said Kana. "You did the right thing."

Kana hadn't looked at Joe while she had pulled off her maneuver, but now she felt his steel grip on her arm, almost lifting her from her seat.

"We've got to go, too," he said to Clem, ushering Kana toward the door. He stopped only long enough to toss money on the counter for the coffee and doughnuts.

Kana's heart was pounding. She was definitely on to something. Jim Granger was in Cajun Corners secretly and Joe Tarwater was furious. It wasn't all she wanted to know, but at least it was a start.

Chapter Twenty-five

Joe drove straight to Silver Mist without a word. Kana knew he was angry with her, but she didn't care. He'd been telling her over and over to trust him, but he didn't trust her enough to tell her what was happening at Silver Mist. Doug and Nicole must be in on it, too. She had thought Nicole was going to tell her when they found the flowers by the door, but Doug had hushed her up. It wasn't like she was asking for confidential information about someone else. She only wanted to know what was going on that was affecting her and Great Pa.

If Joe wouldn't help her, she would have to find out some other way. If he wouldn't be a hundred per cent honest with her, maybe she should slow down and rethink this budding relationship. She had just broken up with one deceitful man. She certainly didn't need to be mixed up with another one. She wished she had someone to talk to about it. She had been able to ask her father and Great Pa anything, but she no longer had them to turn to. She and Sheila had become closer since her father died, but Sheila wasn't there now. Besides, she didn't know what to think when Sheila had gone to the awards with Jim Granger. Maybe she hadn't really been interested in him. Maybe she was only trying to give Kana a wakeup call about the kind of jerk Granger was. It would have hurt less if Sheila had talked to her first. I would have helped if Sheila had talked about a lot of things. There was so much about Sheila that was a mystery!

She decided she'd pay a visit to Oscoe and Fetney Lou when she got back to Silver Mist. They might have some answers. Anyway, it was worth a try.

Joe stopped the car in front of Silver Mist and held Kana's arm like a vise as he escorted her to the door.

"You stay put," he warned gruffly, as if had read her mind. "Don't leave this house until I come back! That's an order!"

"An order?" exclaimed Kana indignantly. "You can't tell me what to do, Joe Tarwater!"

"I'm doing this for your own good," said Joe. "If you set foot outside, I swear I'll put a guard by your door."

He whirled and stormed out the door without another word, or even a look in her direction.

Kana fought back tears. *How could he be so mean and bossy?* She had really begun to think this would work out. Well, it was good to see this side of him before she got more involved. She was eighteen now. She was her own boss. She didn't have to take orders from anyone!

She waited until Joe drove away. Then she ran across the lawn toward the swamp.

Let Joe Tarwater send his guard! She would not be there to be guarded! She refused to be held a prisoner in her own home!

I need to find Fetney Lou, she thought

Kana remembered that the old lady usually spent the days in the swamp gathering herbs. That meant she could be anywhere. Kana wrinkled her brow thoughtfully. Maybe

Oscoe would know where she was. She moved deeper into the swamp.

"Oscoe!" she called. "Fetney Lou? It's Kana! Where are you?"

There was no answer. The silence was eerie. She hadn't noticed until now how quiet it was. Kana had never been easily spooked, but now all her senses were warning her of danger. To her right, a shadow moved among the trees. Something or someone was there watching her. She was overcome with the urge to run from the swamp as fast as she could. A twig snapped nearby and something slithered in the grass beside her.

She didn't wait to see what it was. She ran, and she heard what sounded like a low chuckle behind her. Her heart pounded and her feet fairly flew back to Silver Mist.

She felt very foolish by the time she reached her room. She was gasping for breath and sweat was running down her face. Joe Tarwater would have loved seeing her run like a scared rabbit. She didn't know what had come over her! She'd never run away from anything before.

She tried to rationalize what had happened. Her presence in the swamp had frightened the birds and animals and caused the silence. Her imagination had caused the rest. What she took to be a low chuckle was probably only a bird. Yet she knew she could not go back in there alone. Regardless of what had been watching her – animal or human – it had meant her no good!

She washed her face with a damp cloth and ran a comb through her tousled hair.

She felt better. She had caught her breath and things seemed normal now. She decided this would be a good time to check on Great Pa. It would be wonderful if he could talk to her now.

Nicole was reading in the big chair by his bed when Kana went in. She got up and offered Kana her place.

"I'll take a break if you want to sit with him a while," said Nicole. "He's had a good morning."

"Thanks," said Kana, as she watched Nicole leave the room.

Kana sat by the bed and looked at Great Pa's face. He opened his eyes and saw Kana. She took his hand and smiled. His eyes were clear this morning.

"How are you, Great Pa?" she asked.

"Kana –," he said with a struggle.

"Yes, Great Pa, it's me!" she said. "I'm so glad you know I'm here. I heard you were asking for me. I came as soon as I could."

"Mari-wanna," he said, gasping.

"I don't understand," said Kana. "Who are you talking about? Mary? Wanda? Or is it something you want?"

"No!" said Great Pa, frustrated that the words wouldn't come. He spoke slowly and with great effort. "Mar-I-juana."

"Marijuana?" Kana repeated. That was certainly not what she had expected him to say after four years. She was puzzled. *What was he trying to tell her?*

"Father stop –," said Great Pa. His voice trailed off and he dozed.

Nicole came back into the room.

"Did he speak?" she asked.

"He said a couple of things that didn't make sense," said Kana.

"Like what?" asked Nicole.

"He said something that sounded like marijuana. Then he said father and stop. Do you know what he could have meant?"

Nicole's face turned white. "No," she said, a little too quickly, Kana thought. "He must be confused by his medicine and his dreams."

"Maybe," said Kana.

Nicole could tell she was not convinced.

"I'll stay with him now," said Nicole.

"Since he's sleeping, I think I'll take a nap myself," said Kana.

"Good idea," said Nicole. "The rest will do you good."

Nicole took up her vigil by the bed and began to read her book again.

Kana went to her room and closed the door. She had no intention of sleeping. She waited a few minutes so Nicole would think she was sleeping, though. She decided she would go to the back fields and see for herself what was there. She opened the door and listened. All was quiet as it should be. Kana tiptoed down the back stairs and opened the back door. She bumped into someone as she stepped out. She looked up as Jim Granger smiled down at her.

Chapter Twenty-six

"I can't just sit here and do nothing," said Fetney Lou. "I think I should go to her. I know she's in danger."

"It's her choice, Fetney Lou," said Oscoe. "She needed to do this to grow up completely, maybe to save her soul."

"I'm going to the cypress," she said. "I'll stay out of sight."

"Then I'll go check my traps," said Oscoe. "Remember, this is something she needs to face herself. She has a lot of your strength, you know. I think she may be seeing that for the first time."

"I was wrong about her, Oscoe," said Fetney Lou. "I thought she was selfish. I thought she only thought of herself. I thought her choices made others unhappy and that it didn't matter to her. I realize now that I've been the selfish one. My choices have brought unhappiness to so many, especially to you."

"I made choices of my own," said Oscoe. "I take full responsibility for them. I am glad you let me be a part of your life."

Fetney Lou stood up and moved toward the trees. At the edge of the clearing, she turned and smiled at Oscoe. Then she vanished among the sunlight and the shadows and teeming life of the swamp.

Oscoe stood and decided where to start. He would not go in the same direction. He did not want to intrude. But as always, if Sheila and Fetney Lou needed him, he'd be nearby and ready to comfort or help.

As Oscoe walked away from the cabin, he had no way of knowing that before the day was over, his capacity for giving comfort would be strained to the limit.

Chapter Twenty-seven

Sheila's watch told her she was early for her meeting with Jim Granger. That was good. She was feeling nostalgic. She wanted to look closely at the swamp again.

She spotted an alligator floating unmoving in the water a little way from her.

"That log over there is alive," she said aloud.

She smiled, remembering that Oscoe used to say that to her when they went for walks when she was a child.

She had to look closely to make sure it wasn't a log. She could barely see the edge of its ridgy back and the cold eyes that stared without feeling. It was enough!

"Wicked!" she cried out, and drew back, shuddering. She knew the alligator would keep watching her, and she wanted it to be at a safe distance.

Oscoe was watching, too. In his circle to check his traps, he was surprised to run into her. Sheila saw him and smiled. He smiled back.

"I thought you'd be under the cypress by now," said Oscoe.

"It's still a bit early for Jim," she said. "If he gets there first, he'll wait."

"Want some company?" asked Oscoe.

Sheila nodded. It would be good to have someone to talk to, someone she had walked with, someone who cared about her.

Oscoe remembered their walks, too. She could have been his own child. He wished with all heart that she had been.

"Look!" said Sheila, pointing to the alligator.

"I know," said Oscoe.

"Is my mother all right?" asked Sheila.

"Yes," said Oscoe. "She is strong."

"I love her, you know, in my own way," said Sheila. "And you, too," she added.

"I know," said Oscoe. "I felt the same. But it was hard on her when you went away. She felt lonely and deserted."

"I had to go, Oscoe," said Sheila. "It wasn't because I didn't love her. I had to lead my own life."

"She built her whole life around you," said Oscoe.

"I know," said Sheila. "I used to feel guilty about that. I felt like I cheated her out of the life she wanted by just being born. One day I realized she was feeling guilty, too. She cheated you out of the life you wanted, didn't she, Oscoe?"

"My life was my own choosing, Sheila," he said. "She didn't force me to stay here. My one regret is that she wouldn't marry me when she was carrying you. I could have made her life easier."

"I used to think she and I were so different," said Sheila, "but I know now that's not true. We are really very much alike. She condemned me for wanting to be part of the outside world and going after what I wanted. Yet she did the same thing. She became involved with my father and turned her back on you and life in Cajun Corners. I used to think she was jealous because I succeeded and she didn't, but I believe now that she was afraid for me. She didn't want me to be hurt like she was."

"That's true," said Oscoe. "I'm glad you understand that."

"She has punished herself all these years for her mistake," said Sheila. "She felt she didn't deserve you."

"I forgave her," said Oscoe. "But you are right about the way she felt. She said she wasn't good enough for me. I think she was afraid of a commitment to me after your father deceived her. I think she felt safer in an uncomplicated life."

"I guess you're right," said Sheila, "but it's hard for me to imagine my mother being afraid of anything."

"She's only human," he replied.

"You still love her, don't you?" asked Sheila softly.

"Yes," he said without hesitation. "I always will."

"I'm glad," said Sheila. "If something happens to me, I'll know you are there to look after her and Kana."

"Nothing will happen if you let me tell Joe Tarwater to come here right now," said Oscoe.

Sheila leaned over and kissed the old man's cheek.

"I still have to do things my way!" Sheila said. "I get that from my mother! Maybe I can salvage something from this disaster after all. I made a mistake that I must correct, so I won't have to punish myself for the rest of *my* life."

"Be careful," said Oscoe.

"I'll do my best," Sheila promised.

Sheila smiled and hurried away to the cypress tree. Oscoe watched from the clearing, the alligator watched from the water, and Fetney Lou watched from the shadows as she approached. Let them look, but, for her, there was no looking back.

Chapter Twenty-eight

Fetney Lou concealed herself where she could watch the old tree. She should have done that four years ago to witness the first meeting. Then she would have seen who killed William. If only Great Pa Ulysses could tell them what he saw! Not knowing had been awful! Somehow she knew it would all be revealed today!

While she waited for Sheila, she had watched the white heron come out to feed. She pictured Sheila as a little girl, innocent as the pure white bird.

A woodpecker startled her and made her jump. The meeting should take place soon. She looked at the sky and saw the sun showing mid-morning. A pair of marsh wrens flew over and out of sight. On the river, a man in a pirogue floated silently by on the current. That was a common sight on the bayou.

The sun burned hotter, but the dense growth near the cypress was cool. Spring greenness shimmered around the withered, brown old woman, a study in contrast between the beginning and end of life's circle.

Fetney Lou was close enough to the water to see her reflection when she leaned over. She had been beautiful once, but the hot bayou sun had dried her skin, and pain and loneliness had left their marks.

She heard the snap of a twig. Someone was coming. It wasn't Jim or Sheila. She stood camouflaged, waiting and listening. Fear popped up like beads of sweat along her spine. Someone was here who shouldn't be. Somebody else had come to watch.

Fetney Lou put her trembling hands together and bowed her head. There in nature's temple, she said a prayer to whatever gods there might be.

Chapter Twenty-nine

Kana gasped. The sudden appearance of Jim Granger caught her completely off guard.

"Why, Kana! Aren't you glad to see me?" he asked, putting his hands on her shoulders and sliding them down her arms caressingly.

Kana flinched at his touch. It was repulsive to her now. She tried to step back into the doorway.

Jim held her arms and pretended not to notice. He was far from pleased with her response. He had hoped she had changed her mind about the engagement so he would not have to take further action.

"I–I'm surprised to see you," stammered Kana, telling herself to stay calm. She believed now that she had reason to fear this man and she wanted to avoid an unpleasant confrontation. "I can't believe you're here! I thought you were in Vegas with Sheila."

She was telling the truth in part. She couldn't believe that he'd have the nerve to come here to Silver Mist after she had told him the engagement was off. She knew his coming was more than that. She knew he'd been in town for a while asking questions.

What did he want? His lips were smiling at her now, but

the eyes were cold.

"We have to talk," he said. "Were you headed anywhere in particular just now?"

"J–just for a walk to get some fresh air," said Kana. Instinct warned her not to mention the back fields.

"Then sit with me here on the porch," said Jim. "I won't keep you long. I have some business to take care of with your mother."

"I see," said Kana, allowing him to lead her to the porch swing. So far, the situation seemed harmless enough.

They sat down, but Jim saw the stiffness in her body. She wasn't going to be as easy to handle as he had thought. Well, he would deal with that later. Right now, he wanted to find out how much she had learned from Great Pa.

"Look, Baby," he began. "I know you're sore at me, but we'll work that out later. There are some things going on that you don't know about!"

Kana was so tired of hearing that!

"Oh?" she said sarcastically. "Would you like to tell me what these things are?"

"Yes, I would," he said to her amazement.

She had expected him to ask her to trust him like Joe Tarwater had been doing since they got to Silver Mist.

"Like what things?" she asked cautiously.

"First, Sheila and Nat dreamed up that awards thing for publicity. I had nothing to do with it. I had to go along or lose my job. I had to think of our future, Kana."

"Go on," said Kana, curious about the point he was coming to.

"Second," he continued, "Sheila wasn't trying to keep anything from you about your grandfather. She didn't know. There was no call. Doug and Nicole and their friend

Joe Tarwater have cooked up a scheme to use you, Kana, to get control of Silver Mist and a piece of Sheila's pie, so to speak."

"What on earth are you talking about?" flared Kana. "You are completely crazy and completely wrong!"

"It's true, Kana," he said.

"I don't believe you," said Kana.

"Babe, your cousins only pretended that they told Sheila about your grandfather, but they never said a word to her. Then they wrote you a letter saying they did. They wanted to cause trouble between the two of you. They knew how upset you'd be at Sheila for not telling you something as important as that. Without Sheila on your side, they think they can take your share of Silver Mist for taking care of the old man. Joe Tarwater thinks he can use Sheila to break into the music business big time!"

The whole idea was so absurd that Kana almost laughed.

"I still say you're crazy!" said Kana. "These people aren't like that. They don't think that way!"

"Think about it," he urged. "I came down here secretly and did some digging myself. I came out here last night to confront Doug, but he and Joe Tarwater's guards threw me off the place. I asked to see you, but Doug wouldn't let me. He practically admitted their whole scheme to me, Kana!"

"So that *was* you I saw last night," Kana blurted without thinking.

Jim was glad he had made the admission now that he knew she had seen him. He had considered that possibility. He didn't know how much she had heard, though.

"Then you heard what I said and you know I'm telling you the truth," he continued.

"I didn't hear anything," said Kana. "You were too far

away. I just happened to be going by the window and I saw someone I thought walked like you."

Jim was relieved to hear that she had heard none of the actual conversation. Now he had to try to learn if she knew anything else.

"Kana," he continued smoothly, "I don't like telling you things like this. I know it's hurtful, but I think you should know what you're up against. You must believe me for your own good."

"Why didn't you call me last night?" she asked. "I could have let you in."

"I needed more time to get information about this Tarwater character after last night," Jim told her.

"Now, wait a minute," said Kana. "I've known Joe Tarwater all my life. He'd never be part of a plot like this."

"How *well* do you know him?" asked Jim. "Did you know he wrote songs before he showed up with that tape?"

She had to admit to herself that she hadn't known about Joe's interest in music. It was odd that he hadn't pushed his songs when they were together. Come to think of it, she couldn't remember ever hearing him even hum a tune. Wonder if that tape could have some other purpose? Joe had never said he had songs on it and he never seemed to want her to hear it.

"None of this makes sense," she told Jim.

"Sure it does," he said. "Think about it."

Kana didn't know what to think. She was beginning to feel she couldn't trust anybody, even herself. She had to admit that some of the things Jim said did ring true.

Joe had come into her life again suddenly, and Doug and Nicole had been acting a bit strange. None of them gave her a satisfactory explanation for the things she had seen. And

Joe had even admitted that what he told her about the poachers was a lie.

Jim was pleased to see the confusion in Kana's eyes. He was making progress. He had planted some seeds of doubt. If they took root, maybe she would not have to be killed after all. She was such a pretty little thing. It would be a waste. He still had to learn what, if anything, the old man had told her.

"Jim, what do you know about the lights in the back fields?" Kana asked suddenly.

"There's nothing back there, Kana," he replied without the slightest hesitation. "I've checked the fields myself. They are trying to frighten you away."

Kana remembered the witch's curse left by the back door. Had that really been put there to scare her?

"Kana, it might be safer for you if they don't know that you are aware that there is nothing in the back fields. Maybe you should just stay away from the fields until they've played their hand. Some of those guards looked mean enough to hurt you," he said.

She looked confused. He was sure she was thinking about the things he'd said.

"I've got to go check on Great Pa," said Kana. "I'm sure Nicole is ready for a break."

"Of course," said Jim. "I know you need to be with your grandfather. Has he been able to talk to you yet?"

Kana thought before she spoke this time. She would give no information to anyone that might put Great Pa in danger.

"Ha hasn't said anything that makes any sense," she said. "I think the stroke wiped out his memory of the day my father died."

"I won't keep you any longer," Jim said in his most charming voice. "You will want to be there if he wakes up.

I will call you after I meet with Sheila. She is coming here to tell you the truth. I hope you'll listen to her."

Kana nodded, relieved to get away and be alone.

"And Kana," Jim said, as he stood to go. "When I see you again, I hope you will be wearing my ring."

He walked to his car without waiting for her answer. He smiled as he drove away. Maybe he could still convince her. He still wanted to marry her and get control of Sheila's millions. That would be the easiest way. For now he would let her live.

Kana climbed the stairs in a daze. The phone rang and Nicole came out of Great Pa's room to answer it. She didn't see Kana in the hall.

Kana went to Great Pa's door and looked in. He was awake! He motioned to her and she hurried to the bed.

Kana knelt beside the bed.

"Great Pa," she whispered, "I don't know what to do! I wish you could tell me who to believe!"

He took her hand and pulled her close. In a low, clear voice, he began to speak. In amazement, Kana listened to every word!

Chapter Thirty

Jim headed his car in the direction of the airport in case Kana was watching. Then he turned on the old road that led to the swamp. He hid the car among the trees at the edge and headed into the swamp on foot. Limbs scraped his arms and shoulders and sweat trickled down his neck. He longed for his plush air-conditioned office in Nashville, but he made himself keep walking.

Sheila had stopped to rest and saw an alligator watching her again. Was it the same one she and Oscoe had seen? Surely not! She forced herself to move toward the cypress as the sun climbed higher.

Fetney Lou wiped her brow with the hem of her petticoat. She ate ripe strawberries from her pocket and that refreshed her somewhat. From far across the bayou came a loud rumble of thunder.

"That's the Devil talking," said Fetney Lou.

Another angry rumble followed the first.

Oscoe heard it, too, from his hiding place near the tree. He had taken a short cut after talking to Sheila, so he'd be set before she arrived. He hoped the storm would hold off for a while. It sounded like a violent one. The branches trembled slightly in fear of the wind. It was a bad omen.

Jim Granger heard the thunder, too. He hoped Sheila would be on time. He didn't want to be stuck in the swamp in a thunderstorm!

Sheila watched the sun dim as the dark cloud rolled closer. A spring storm in the swamp could be deadly. She took a deep breath and began to run!

Chapter Thirty-one

At Silver Mist, the rumble of thunder did not drown out the old man's words.

"I must tell you," he said to Kana. "I can't take this with me to my grave."

Kana watched him struggle to make the right words come quickly.

"Take your time, Great Pa," said Kana. "I won't leave until you tell me what you want me to know."

"The day your father died, he found drug crops in the back fields," he told her. "Met Jim Granger by the old tree. Told Jim to get drugs out."

His breathing was becoming harder.

"Relax, Great Pa," Kana told him, but she was hardly breathing herself. She was finally going to find out the truth about her father's death.

"They argued, " the old man continued. "Jim pulled a gun. Just then Sheila headed to the tree to meet your father. Saw alligator. Screamed!"

The old man stopped and closed his eyes. Kana thought he was drifting off again, but he opened his eyes and continued.

"Both men jumped and looked in her direction. I thought

I could get the gun. I grabbed Jim from behind. Gun went off. My son was dead."

"Oh, my Lord, no!" said Kana.

"It's true," said the old man. "I killed your father."

"Oh, Great Pa!" sobbed Kana.

Tears stood in the old man's eyes. "Sheila didn't see it," he said, "Jim ran away. My head exploded inside. God forgive me!"

Through her tears, Kana saw his body relax. He took a deep breath and then there was none at all.

"No, Great Pa!" Kana cried. "Please don't die!"

Blindly, she ran to the door, pushing aside Nicole, who had returned from the phone in time to hear the whole thing. Kana ran outside and headed toward the back fields. She had to see the crops growing there herself. She cut through the swamp, oblivious to the low limbs that clawed at her. The clouds were dark and close, but Kana didn't notice.

Nicole screamed for Doug.

"He's gone," she sobbed when Doug rushed in.

Over her shoulder, he could see the still, peaceful face of his grandfather. There was nothing more he could do for him.

"Where's Kana?" he asked.

"She ran out toward the swamp," said Nicole, still sobbing. "To the back fields. Oh, God, Doug! He told her that he was the one who killed William!"

"What?" exclaimed Doug.

"It was an accident! He was trying to get Jim's gun," she explained. "I heard it all from the doorway. I didn't want to intrude. Then he stopped breathing and Kana tore out of here like a crazy person."

"Why was she in here alone?" asked Doug.

"I went to answer the phone," said Nicole. "I thought Kana was taking a nap. Joe Tarwater called to say he'd learned that Sheila is meeting Jim Granger at that old tree this morning. They should be there now. He said he was going there and we should keep Kana away. When I got back to the door, Kana was kneeling by his bed and he just started talking. When he died, she ran by me – nearly knocked me down. I couldn't stop her!"

"I've got to find her," said Doug. "That storm is coming fast and it's a bad one. Call the sheriff and tell him about Great Pa. He'll need to send the coroner out."

"Be careful, Doug," she pleaded. "I hate these storms!"

She watched him run across the lawn to the truck while the clouds whirled above him like a wild Cajun dancer.

Chapter Thirty-two

Lightning streaked ahead of Joe Tarwater as he pulled his car onto the old swamp road. He saw Jim Granger's car where he had tried to conceal it among the trees.

Thunder boomed and a streak of lightning cracked like a whip. Joe could see by the swirling clouds that the wind would get stronger. At least Kana was safe at Silver Mist.

Joe left his car by a clump of willows and ran up the path on foot. Then he cut through the trees, hoping to arrive at the old cypress unseen.

Sheila saw no one by the tree as she approached it. The wind was picking up now and she was frightened. Twigs and leaves were beginning to whirl thick in the air.

Kana felt the first drops of rain when the cypress tree came in sight. The drops mixed with her tears as she stopped short, staring at the figure by the tree. The rain and tears blurred her vision at first, but as it cleared, she realized the figure by the tree was Sheila. If Jim had gone to the airport to pick her up, then how could she be here? How, indeed, unless he had lied as she suspected!

Sheila saw Kana at the same moment. She held out her arms and Kana ran into them.

"I'm sorry," sobbed Kana. "I love you! I really do! I always have."

"I know, Honey," said Sheila. "I love you, too!"

"So much has happened," said Kana. "Great Pa just told me that he accidentally killed father. Then he died!"

Kana began to sob harder and Sheila held her close and let her cry.

"I'm so sorry, Kana," she said, "but everything will be all right."

"I don't know who to trust!" said Kana.

"Not Jim Granger!" said Sheila emphatically.

Neither had heard the footsteps behind them. Jim Granger had stepped to the trunk of the old hollow cypress and was leaning against it.

"Isn't this a touching reunion?" he sneered. "I told you what would happen if you double crossed me, Sheila."

Sheila saw the gun he was holding, and she quickly stepped in front of Kana. She looked him straight in the eye.

"You don't frighten me anymore," she said calmly. "It's over. You and your men are out."

"Drop your gun," ordered Joe Tarwater, stepping out into the clearing. "Now!"

Jim Granger threw back his head and laughed. A clap of thunder jarred the ground as a spear of lightning plunged into the old cypress. Jim's laugh turned to a shriek as the shattered tree and Jim Granger merged into one towering flame!

Sheila screamed, and her body crumpled to the ground. Kana felt a tingling throughout her body from the shock. She struggled to stand up, as she felt herself falling backward. Her foot caught in the roots of a giant mangrove tree and she pitched toward the water. She saw Sheila on her knees, and with horror she saw an alligator break the surface of the water in front of her.

Doug had reached the clearing as the bolt struck. He saw Kana fall and he saw the alligator. He took out his gun, but he had no chance to shoot.

"No!" screamed Fetney Lou, dashing from her hiding place toward her granddaughter. She was not quick enough.

Oscoe's arms reached out and held her back. She had not known he was so close. She struggled, but he wouldn't let go.

For an instant, Kana and the alligator were frozen in mid-air. Joe raced toward them, but Sheila was on her feet, shoving Kana back from the bank into Joe's arms. Kana reached for her mother, but she couldn't hold on. Sheila's feet slipped on the rain-slick moss that gave no traction. She slid into the water as the greedy jaws of the alligator snapped shut like a trap. The world went black as Kana sank into unconsciousness.

Doug and Joe fired at the same time. The thrashing in the water continued as they fired and fired again and again. The river water turned red like the flaming tree.

Chapter Thirty-three

Nicole stood at the window and watched the storm while she waited for the sheriff. She saw the blaze among the trees and prayed that Doug and the others were safe.

She heard the siren of the sheriff's car, and she saw car lights coming from the swamp. She hurried down to open the door.

She saw Joe's car first. He lifted Kana in his arms and carried her toward the house. Fetney Lou and Oscoe got out of the back seat and followed. Doug' struck pulled in behind Joe's car and Nicole cried with relief. She saw no sign of Sheila or Jim Granger.

The moments that followed were filled with disbelief. She listened with horror as Doug told her about Sheila and Jim.

She had to do something. She had to touch something normal. She made coffee and fixed hot soup and sandwiches. The storm let up, but the rain set in for the night.

The sheriff came with the coroner. Then the undertaker came and took Great Pa away. Doug followed to make the arrangements for the funeral. Oscoe took Fetney Lou home.

When Joe had placed Kana on her bed, he turned to Nicole and said, "Take good care of her for me." Then he left for the back fields with the sheriff. Jim's guards would be gone, but the crops would have to be destroyed.

Nicole took off Kana's wet clothes and put her to bed. Dr. Blanton had come and gone. He assured Nicole that Kana would be okay. Doug called to tell her he had made arrangements for Great Pa and Sheila, too. He hoped it would be okay with Kana. He was going to the back fields to help destroy the crops before coming home.

Nicole pulled a chair close to Kana's bed and cried herself to sleep. She didn't wake up until much later when Joe Tarwater shook her gently so he could take her place.

Chapter Thirty-four

Joe's face was the first thing Kana saw when she opened her eyes. She began to weep silently. He sat on the edge of the bed and held her in his arms a long, long time.

"I'm sorry," he said simply.

"Sheila?" asked Kana. "Is she–?"

"Dead," he nodded.

She wept again and he held her and rocked her while she cried. Then he told her everything he couldn't tell her before. Finally, from sheer exhaustion, she slept.

Her dreams were filled with images of red water and alligators. She saw Oscoe and Fetney Lou close by when Doug and Joe lifted Sheila's remains from the water. It was the worst thing she could imagine seeing, but out of the nightmare came the knowledge of how much her mother really loved her. She saw the old tree devoured by hungry flames. The sounds of Jim's shriek, of the gun shots, and the rage of the storm made her cry out in her sleep, but Joe's arms were there for her.

Joe left her side long enough to shower and handle the swarms of reporters and photographers that covered every angle of the grisly sight.

Kana refused to see anyone. Nicole brought her hot soup

and a sandwich, but she wouldn't eat. She got out of bed and stared at the back fields from her window. The day finally ended.

Joe came in at dark with a tray. There was more soup and steaming coffee.

"Eat, Kana, " he ordered. This time, she did.

"Sheila saved my life," said Kana.

"Yes," said Joe.

"I don't understand why she was willing to die for me when she wasn't willing to tell the world that I was her daughter," said Kana.

"I think you'd better read this," said Joe, handing her the letter Sheila had mailed to him.

Kana read silently. He could see that some of the things shocked her. Sheila had spared no details and made no excuses in her letter. She wrote of her need for fame and her music, and her selfish pursuit of that. She wrote of William's and Fetney Lou's need for privacy and time with Kana. She told of the songs he wrote for her and his desire to stay out of the spotlight. She explained how one lie led to another and another. She told of the joy she'd experienced by having Kana with her on the road after William died and how she had finally had grown up!

"Don't build your life on deceit, Kana," she wrote. "It will destroy your dreams and those you love if you do. I should never have let Jim Granger blackmail me. I should never have let him get a foothold at Silver Mist or a chance to get at you. I love you more than life itself. I hope you will always remember the love and try to forget my mistakes."

"I should share this with Fetney Lou," said Kana.

"Sheila left a letter for her, too," said Joe. "Your grandmother wants to talk to you when you feel better."

"Sheila said she wrote a song of her own," said Kana. "I wish I could hear it."

"The CD will be released soon," said Joe. "This is what she wrote for the insert." He handed Kana another sheet of paper to read.

"Oh, Joe!" she said. "She dedicated her song to her mother, Fetney Lou, and her daughter, Kana. In the end, she didn't care what the fans thought!"

"That's right," said Joe. "And the irony is that there are already advance orders for this CD that indicate it will be her biggest seller ever! We found a tape among her things at Fetney Lou's. It's 'Sheila's Song.' Are you up to hearing it?"

"Yes, please!" Kana nodded.

He turned on the tape player and came and sat by Kana.

Sheila's voice filled the room – the clear, pure voice Kana had heard and loved as a child. She could see Sheila as she had been then, and that image helped blot out the last one. Kana leaned her head on Joe's shoulder and gave herself up to the music.

My mother was a snowy heron,
And, like her, I will soar on the wind.
No peak is too high
As I reach for the sky,
And I pray I will never descend!
I love the might
Of the dizzying height!
I want to go where I never have been!
My mother was a snowy heron
And, like her, I will soar on the wind.

Kana was silent for a long time after the song ended.

"You know, Joe," she said finally. "I've been thinking that I'd like to give Doug and Nicole my share of Silver Mist. And I'd like to spend some time with my grandmother."

"You can do both," said Joe. "Your new home is next door with me."

"Really?" said Kana. "Joe Tarwater, are you asking me to marry you?"

"Yes," Joe answered.

"But you told me I shouldn't marry the first man who asked me," said Kana.

"I'm not the first," he said. "I'm the second."

"Well, in that case," laughed Kana, "you can consider it settled."

As Joe kissed Kana, a white heron called in the swamp. Kana could have sworn she heard Sheila's voice far away — a faint strain of heavenly music soaring on the wind.